G STREET CHRONICLES PRESENTS

ESSENCE OF A Bad Girl

Mz. Robinson

Published by G Street Chronicles
P.O. Box 490082
College Park, GA 30349

www.gstreetchronicles.com
Fan@gstreetchronicles.com

Cover Design:
Cupcake Creative Studios
vondahoward@me.com

Typesetting & Ebook Conversion:
G&S Typesetting & Ebook Conversion
info@gstypesetting.com

LCCN: 2010932926
ISBN: 978-09826543-2-3

Join us on Facebook G Street Chronicles Fan Page

Other books

by

Mz. Robinson

Visit www.gstreetchronicles.com
to view all our titles

Join us on Facebook
G Street Chronicles Fan Page

Mz. Robinson's

Love

Lust

&

Lies

Series

Octavia Ellis is a sexy and independent woman who plays it safe when it comes down to relationships. She lives by one rule: keep it strictly sexual. Octavia is living her life just the way she wants. No man. No issues. No drama. When she meets the handsome Damon Whitmore, everything changes. Octavia soon finds that Damon has become a part of her world and her heart. However, when temptation comes in the form of a sexy-hardcore thug named, Beau, Octavia finds herself caught in a deadly love triangle. She soon learns in life and love, there are no rules and she's surprised at what she herself, will not do for love.

Mz. Robinson's

Love Lust & Lies Series

Shontay Holloway is as faithful as they come when it comes to her husband, Kenny. For eight years she's been his support system physically and financially. She's managed to overlook the fact that he's a woman chaser and even turned the other cheek when he got another woman pregnant. Shontay would rather work it out with Kenny than start fresh with someone new. She's not satisfied but she is content. Is there really a difference? Shontay doesn't think so, but that soon changes when she meets Savoy Breedwell.

Shontay finds herself torn between her vows and the man she's falling for. When tragedy strikes, Shontay learns that the love she thought her husband had for her is nothing more than a cover up for his true intentions. She becomes a woman on a mission. When she's finished, Till death do us part, may have a whole new meaning.

Coming October 2011 Part 3

Love Lust & Lies Series

"What would you do for love?"
"How would you handle the discovery that your marriage was built on lies?"

Damon Whitmore is a true go-getter who will stop at nothing to get what he desires. His wife Octavia was no exception. When Damon first saw Octavia he knew he had to have her. He went through great lengths until his mission was accomplished. Now, two years later, he and Octavia share a wonderful and lavish life together. Damon exceeded all of Octavia's expectations while managing to keep his secrets of deceit and manipulation hidden but what's done in the dark eventually comes to light and Damon's lies are slowly beginning to unravel.

When a face from Damon's past re-surfaces, Damon finds himself facing a life alerting dilemma that could cause him to lose the very thing he fought so hard to build—his family with Octavia. Damon refuses to lose and he'll stop at nothing, including murder, to keep his family in tact.

Octavia Ellis-Whitmore never thought she would be a one man woman. Living by a no strings attached policy, she kept her encounters with men strictly sexual. When she met Damon everything in her world changed. Octavia opened her heart and fell hard for Damon. Octavia is now living and loving her life to the fullest. However, history has a way of repeating itself and temptation has a way of finding Octavia. When things at home begin to get rocky, Octavia finds herself struggling between remaining true to the vows she pledged to Damon and exploring her feelings for a new and mysterious stranger—a stranger who has a startling connection to Damon and his past.

As the drama unfolds, lies and secrets will be exposed and lines will be crossed on both ends. How far will Damon and Octavia go to protect each other from the other's transgressions and how many will fall victim to the lies that have been spun in the name of love?

ESSENCE OF A
Bad Girl

Mz. Robinson's Dedications

This book is dedicated to my bestie, Banita Green-Brooks. Banita, through thick and thin you have been there to offer advice, make me laugh, and give me a reality check when needed. A real friend stands with you when you're up and extends a hand to you when you're down. That's exactly what you've always done for me.

I am truly blessed that God sent me a friend and a sister when he sent you. You're a bad chick who takes care of her family, looks out for her friends, and has no problem helping a stranger. Thank you for being real. I love you!

"Real women don't beg for attention…
they command it."

Mz. R

Acknowledgements

To the Alpha and the Omega, my Lord and Savior, thank you for continuing to shine your grace and mercy upon me. I am so grateful and I am nothing without you. To my parents Ray and Shirley, your love and continued support are a blessing. Thank you for always believing in me and reminding me that I can do anything I put my heart and mind into. The two of you have sacrificed so much to stand by me and I promise your giving shall not be in vain. You are my angels and I love you both beyond words.

To my beautiful cousin Tammy Walker, I love you and thank you for the encouragement and the advice. I heard you and took in every single word. To my cousin Jeffery Massey, thank you for the support and always offering a smile. I love you. To my Aunt Mable, my cousin Sonya, and the entire Massey family, I love you all and thank you for believing in me! To my families, the Caudle & Warner Families: Thank you for purchasing each and every book and showing so much love and support. I love you all! To my cousin Amanda, thank you for the love and spreading the word. I love you! To my cousin Quiana, I'm so glad we connected (even if it was on FB..Lol), I love you! To my girls: Valerie Ann Williams and Deloris, you two are always willing to grind, thank you! To my adoptive mother, Ms. JoAnn, I love you and thank you for believing in me. To all the ladies at Wal-Mart Store# 433 and the Huntsville Hospital Team who showed me love and support by pre-ordering and purchasing my books, thank you. To Mankumar and Mani, thank you for reading and spreading the word! To Anthony Conley at Expansion Books, thank you so much! To every book store, book club, reader, reviewer, and fan, thank you from the bottom of my heart! To George Sherman Hudson, Ceo of G Street Chronicles, everything happens for a reason and although I may never understand why God directed our paths to cross, I am so very glad he did. When getting published was only a dream you helped make it a reality. Thank you for teaching me this game and offering a kind word when I thought I could not go on. It means more to me than you will ever know. Love & Respect to you Always! Shout out to Author Khaream Gibson, thank you for promoting. Feb 2011 is coming, Two Face…Get 'em! To the rest of G Street Chronicles' authors both old and new, much love. To my editor, Autumn Conley Bittick, thank you! To Vonda Howard, thank you for yet another hot cover!

"To everyone with a hope and a dream,
a wish and a prayer,
keep P.U.S.H.I.N.G!"

~ *Kisses Mz. Robinson*

Prologue

I stand admiring Barron in silence. He's pretty in a masculine kind of way. From his dark skin to his regal nose and high cheekbones, Barron has features suitable for a runway model. Looking at Barron lying butt naked across the king-sized bed, I can't help but smile. The man is beautiful, absolutely fine. At six-one and 230 pounds, he looks more like a Dallas Cowboy than an auto mechanic. Another thing I love about Barron is that he definitely knows how to treat a woman. He's attentive, charming, and a complete gentleman. In addition to being well mannered, he's a very hard worker. Any woman who ends up with Barron by her side will be a lucky lady. It's too bad I'm already spoken for. If I were able to give my heart to Barron, I could definitely see us being happy. I can see it now:

the cute little house with the privacy fence, two kids, a dog and a couple of goldfish—the perfect middle-class family. Middle class? The thought jolts me back to the harsh reality. I grew up poor, and in my opinion, middle class is just one unpaid bill away from being broke.

He gives me that sweet, perfect smile I've grown accustom to over the last eight months and then extends his hand to me. I walk slowly across the carpeted floor and then, like a little girl reaching out to her daddy, I slip my hand into his. His hand is warm and soft despite the calluses he's earned from working so hard. Pulling me down onto the bed, he shifts slightly so my head is resting on the soft garden of hair that carpets his broad chest. "Did you enjoy the show?" he asks, stroking my hair with his fingertips.

"Yes," I answer sincerely. After treating me to dinner, Barron took me to see a local performance of *What We Won't Do for Love,* a play based on a novel by a chick that calls herself Mz. Robinson. Maybe it was the storyline or simply the fact that Barron was there with me, but whatever it was, I truly enjoyed myself. Sometimes the little things really do mean a lot to me.

"Do you really have to leave tomorrow?" he asks.

Here we go, I think to myself. I already informed Barron earlier that I am leaving, but I forgot to mention we will never see each other again. "Yes," I say.

I feel his arms tightening around me. Although, the words have never been spoken, I know he loves me. There are some things a woman can read in a man, even when they are left unspoken.

"When will you be back?" he asks.

"I'm not sure," I lie. I don't have the heart to tell him the truth. I have no intention of returning to Huntsville, no intention of ever seeing Barron again, no intention of ever again riding the ten inches of solid manhood I now feel pressing against the pit of my stomach. But I can't tell him any of this. I know it would hurt him, and despite the fact that I have been dishonest with him from day one, I can't bring myself to see the pain in his eyes.

"I wish you would just stay here," he continues. His voice, which is normally a deep, sultry baritone, has become soft, almost soprano. "I can take care of you," he promises. "You can let me be your sole provider."

Inside, I laugh at the thought. Barron's three-bedroom apartment could never be big enough for me. His two-door Lincoln Continental could never give me the adrenaline rush I need, and sadly enough, his eighteen-dollar-an-hour job could never fund my shoe fetish. I need the finer things in life, and what Barron fails to realize or is unaware of is that I already have these things—only not with him.

The home waiting for me in Atlanta resembles a

miniature mansion, with five bedrooms, six full baths, a heated swimming pool with a grotto, an indoor gym, a home theater, a library, and a five-car garage. Inside the impressive garage rest my Aston Martin DB9, Cadillac Escalade, and Lexus IS250. The funding for my home and my cars came from the man waiting for me there, my fiancé, Andrew Carlton. So, although Barron is a sweetheart and is offering me a deal many women would jump at, I must sadly decline. I have too much waiting for me at home to throw it all away on a gentleman with some fire dick. Still, I have to let him down easy. "Baby, I can't let you do that," I purr, pulling myself up so I'm straddling him. I'm in the perfect position to slide down onto his erection, but I want to make him wait. I don't want to break Barron's heart, but teasing him is something I'm not opposed to.

"I know, I know." His breathing becomes deep and ragged. His brown eyes are screaming for me to let him in, pleading me to let him feel the heat and wetness of my always ready pot of gold. "Miss Independent," he moans while squeezing my phat apple bottom.

"That's right, Daddy." I dip my head down to his neck. Blowing lightly just below his right ear lobe, I began to move slowly, grinding my kitty against his stomach, just above the thick head of his chocolate rod.

"But I—"

I silence his words with my lips. Kissing him softly, I allow his tongue to enter my mouth and find mine. We kiss with animalistic desire—the kind of desire shared by two people who can never be together, never be free to belong only to one and another. His lips move from mine down to my neck, then to my ear, and back to my lips again. I can feel his heart beating like an African drum in the middle of the jungle. My temperature is rising, and although I consider myself a huntress, I feel like the prey. I lift my hips just enough to allow him to enter me, and Barron wastes no time. He thrust his hips up, forcing his rock hard dick up inside of me. I clench the muscles of my pussy, gripping him tightly.

"Mmm…"

Hearing him moan only fuels the fire burning inside of me. I bounce up and down, up and down, causing my ass to jiggle wildly. Grabbing my cheeks roughly with both hands, Barron forces me to change my rhythm. I now began to rock backwards and then forward on his pipe. He opens his full lips while staring into my eyes. I grab his head, bringing his ready mouth to my full, round breast. Barron latches onto my protruding nipple like a hungry newborn with a fresh bottle. The sound of him sucking on me mingled with the swishing of my wetness makes me hotter. I dig my manicured nails into his bulging biceps, almost causing his skin to tear. "Fuck me harder!" I scream.

Barron sits up, cradling me in his lap, and then in one swift movement, he has me on my stomach with my face pressed against the bed. My pulse is racing from the anticipation of the pleasure-filled pain he is about to give me. Barron is a lot like me when it comes to sex; he likes it hard—in fact, the harder the better. Grabbing a handful of my hair, Barron pulls my head back. I push up onto my knees, arching my back and elevating my ass. I can feel his solid chest against my back, the warmth of his body.

"Now!" I gasp, breathing heavily.

"Now what?" he grumbles. He teases me, rubbing his dick back and forth across my ass. The simple action sends tingles down my spine. Tracing his tongue down the nape of my neck, then across the blade of my shoulder, Barron continues to taunt me. "Now what?!" His voice is deep, almost angry, and I love it.

"Give it to me now," I whisper.

He eases inside of me slowly, feeding me inch by inch. He rotates his hips seductively; I rotate mine in return, matching his rhythm, and then he stops.

"Don't stop!" I beg. "Please!"

"Please what?" he snaps.

"Please, Barron."

"Please who?" he asks, slapping me hard on the ass.

The force causes my cheek to sting.

"Barron…" I repeat, and he slaps my butt harder. I flinch from the pain. A low moan escapes my lips.

"Please who?" he asks, grabbing me by the waist.

I can no longer take the anticipation. I'm ready. "Please, Daddy!"

Barron dives inside me with violent force. The impact of our bodies connecting pushes me chest first across the feather pillows into the oak headboard.

"Yes! Yes!" I scream. I close my eyes and exhale as Barron drills, grinds, and beats my pussy from the back.

* * * * *

Three hours later, I stand in Barron's bathroom surveying the damage to my body. I have bruises on my breast and my ass. The purple marks look out of place against my caramel skin. Aside from a birthmark underneath my right breast and a small scar on my left ankle, my body is flawless. At twenty-seven, I have a body that would make an eighteen-year-old envious: perfect round D-cup breasts, wide hips, and an ass that would give Deelishis a run for her money. Along with the body, I have the looks: a heart-shaped face with big brown eyes; long, curly eyelashes; thick, full eyebrows; smooth, full lips; and thick, jet-black, shoulder-length hair. I have the body and the face, and I know how to use them.

I get dressed quickly and quietly, as I don't want to wake Barron. I've grown fond of him over the past few months, and because I know I will soon bring him pain, I still can't look him in the eyes. As I walk toward the bed, I secretly wish things could be different, but it is what it is. We make our beds, and we have to lie in them.

Barron's chest rises and falls gently with the intake and exhale of every breath. I touch his face softly and gently kiss his full lips. He moves slightly from my touch and then continues to sleep peacefully. I quickly slip out of his bedroom and then the front door. *I'll miss my beautiful prince*, I tell myself as one door closes another one prepares to open.

Chapter 1

(Essence)

I had barely wiped the crud out of my eyes, when the phone began to ring. Rolling over onto my side, I shot an angry glace at the digital alarm clock that was resting on the nightstand: the digital 6:45 stood out like a red beacon in the night sky. "Are you serious?!" I grumbled, clearing my throat. "It's Saturday, for crying out loud." Reaching past the alarm clock, I snatched the cordless phone out of its cradle. Whomever was on the other line was about to get a well-deserved verbal beat down.

"Let it ring."

I looked over my shoulder to see Andrew's charcoal grey eyes staring at me. He gave me a warm smile that instantly caused my anger to subside. Andrew had that effect on me. In an instant, with just once glance, he could make me forget whoever or whatever was bothering me. It was one of the many things I loved about him and another reason I was thankful he loved me.

When I met Andrew, his eyes were one of the first things I noticed about him. I was sitting in Starbucks enjoying my typical white chocolate cappuccino when I noticed two beautiful eyes staring at me over the top of the *Atlanta Daily*. Just when I smiled, he lowered the paper to reveal one of the most beautiful men I had ever laid eyes on. He had low-cut black wavy hair; gray eyes with long, dark lashes; a round baby face with high cheek bones; and skin the color of brown sugar. There was a perfectly trimmed mustache resting below his wide nose, accentuating his full 'lick me dry' mouth. I had yet to get over how exotic and perfect his face was when he stood and almost took my breath away. He was six-three, dressed in a professionally tailored pinstripe suit with a body that screamed 'Damn, I'm fine!' He walked over to my table, introduced himself, and sat down without an invitation except the one he must have seen in my eyes.

The two of us instantly hit it off. We discovered we had quite a bit in common, including our love of art and music. Also, we had both grown up in the foster care system. We sat and talked for hours, and the rest is history.

Relaxing, I rolled over so we were lying eye to eye.

"Good morning, beautiful." He smiled, opening his arms.

"Good morning." I snuggled into his warm embrace and rested my head on his bare chest. The aroma of Shea butter and sandalwood teased my senses. "You smell good, even after sleeping," I mumbled, running my fingers over his smooth chest.

"Thank you," he chuckled lightly.

"I'm serious," I said, looking up at him. "I've never met a man who wakes up smelling as good as he did when he went to sleep."

"You've never met a man like me." He smiled and then kissed me gently on the forehead. Before I could agree with him, our conversation was interrupted by the phone, ringing again.

"Who do you think it is?" I asked, exhaling loudly.

"Probably someone wanting to schedule an interview," he teased.

"Oh, please...not another interview," I whined.

The two of us had granted at least ten interviews in the past two weeks since we announced our engagement and had several more scheduled in the weeks to come.

"You're the one who wanted to go public with our engagement," he reminded me.

Andrew was right. The two of us had been together

for two years, and up until two weeks earlier, I was non-existent. There were always rumors Andrew was dating someone, but outside of his publicist and inner circle, no one knew that someone was me. Our decision to keep our involvement on the down-low was my request. If the decision had been left solely up to Andrew, I would have been on the red carpet with him from day one, but I wanted to keep a low profile—for good reason. My past was more checkered than a NASCAR flag, and there was no way I wanted to risk being exposed to Andrew. When Andrew proposed to me, everything changed. Yes, I would be scared pissless if Andrew found out about the skeletons in my closet, but I longed to be there for him in the public eye. I figured if God was kind enough to send me a man as wonderful and loving as Andrew, somewhere along the line He must have granted me pardon for all my transgressions. It was that hope that helped me believe the people I had wronged in the past would not be back to haunt me as ghosts in the present.

I snapped myself out of the mental daydream to answer. “I know,” I sighed.

“Do you regret it now?”

“No,” I said, sincerely. “It’s just overwhelming sometimes.”

“I know, babe,” he said, running his fingertips gently down my spine. I shook slightly from the sensation. “I’ll tell Simone to reschedule all the others," he said. "That'll give you some time to regroup."

Simone was Andrew's publicist and longtime friend. The two of them had an ongoing business relationship for eight years. Until Andrew and I met, Simone was his go-to girl for everything. She not only took care of his publicity, but she also cooked and cleaned for him. In fact, she had her own personal bedroom in Andrew's home. Andrew swore nothing had ever happened between the two of them, but I knew his version of 'nothing' could very well be completely different from hers. Nevertheless, I didn't dwell on whether or not they had sex. As long as it didn't happen after I was in the picture, it just wasn't important to me. I had no fear that Andrew had feelings for Simone. However, it was obvious from the day Simone and I met that she wanted to be more than just Andrew's friend. There was something about the way she looked at him, about the way she stared at me like a jealous lover, that gave her away. I've never been an insecure woman. Why would I? I'm five-five, a light 120 pounds, with caramel skin, D-cups, luscious wide hips, and booty worthy of a video shoot. Simone was definitely not my competition, but I wasn't going to take any chances. That's why when Andrew and I decided we were going to be exclusive, I politely excused Simone from her domestic duties. She voiced her complaint to Andrew, as I assume she thought he would take her side and she would still be running around playing the happy housewife, but she assumed wrong. Andrew stood behind me, and I was granted the keys to his luxurious home, while Simone was demoted to handling only the scheduling of his appearances and interviews.

"Could you please?" I pleaded sweetly.

"Consider it done."

"Thanks, boo!" I smiled then moved my body so I was straddling him. Dipping my head, I pressed my lips to his. It was a simple, sweet kiss, but it was enough to get my blood flowing. Sliding my hand underneath me, I stroked him gently through his silk pajama pants. Andrew let out a low moan. Leaning down, I trailed kisses down the curve of his neck.

"Mmm, baby," he moaned.

I continued to massage his growing manhood while gently nibbling and sucking on his earlobe.

"You know exactly what to do."

"Yes, and I know exactly what I want," I said, pulling my silk negligee up over my head and throwing it down onto the floor.

Andrew's eyes traveled from my face down to my full breast. Squeezing them gently, he licked his lips before taking my tight nipple in his mouth. Andrew licked and sucked my chocolate peak with seductive gentleness. In between my legs, I could feel my heated juices gathering. In one swift movement, he rolled me onto my back, spreading my legs with his strong shoulders.

"Yes," I moaned, as his lips covered my tingling clit.

Andrew sucked my clit slowly and gently before slipping his warm tongue into my watery kitty.

"Right there, baby," I whispered, rotating my hips.

Andrew made love to me with his skilled tongue until I exploded into a waterfall of creamy ecstasy. My body continued to tremble as Andrew slipped his pants off and entered me slowly. I spread my legs until I was in a full split; I loved being flexible. For one, it turned Andrew on, and for two, it allowed me to feel every rock hard inch he had to work with. Andrew rotated his hips, with every motion diving deeper in to my soaking wet pussy. "I love you," he moaned, kissing me softly on the lips.

"I love you, too, baby," I said. I felt his body tense and his legs shake. Increasing our rhythm, we moved as one until he came, exploding inside of me.

After a brief moment of lying in each other's arms in silence, Andrew finally said, "I have to meet Carlito at the office this morning."

"Oh? So you're just going to hit it and leave? Wham, bam, thank you ma'am?" I said, sitting up to face him.

"Never that," he said, stroking my hair gently. "I'll

always come back to you."

"Umm.. hmm," I pouted, folding my arms across my breasts.

"When I get back, we'll do anything you want," he assured me, kissing me softly on the neck. "Dinner?" he whispered, tracing his lips down to my shoulder. "Dancing?" he continued.

I rolled my eyes and then sucked my teeth dramatically. I was disappointed Andrew and I were not going to be making the headboard knock all morning, but I knew he had to handle business.

As the starting quarterback for the Atlanta Fire and the owner of Carlton and Carlton Media, he was constantly on the go—not that I minded. I've always loved a man with ambition and drive. There's nothing more irritating than a man with no hustle and too much time on his hands.

"Shopping?" he whispered, flicking his tongue along my bottom lip.

"Umm.."

"Anywhere you want."

"Milan?" I asked, daring him to say no.

"Then Milan it is," he promised, "but just not today."

He gave me another quick peck on the lips before he climbed out of bed. I was lying sprawled out on my back, watching him put together his ensemble for the day, when the phone rang yet again.

"Can you get that, babe?" he asked as he walked to the master bathroom.

"I guess so!" I laughed, rolling back over to my side of the bed. I picked up the cordless handset. The caller ID showed read 'Unknown'. "Hello?" I said.

"Hello, Tatiana."

"I'm sorry? What did you say?" I asked, thinking I had heard the man on the other end incorrectly.

"I said hello," he laughed. "Tatiana."

"You have the wrong number," I said quickly. The sound of my heart beating rapidly echoed in my ears.

"I'm sorry." His voice was low and harsh, as if his vocal cords had been damaged from years of smoking. "I'm sure the number is right, but what name do you prefer?" he asked.

"Who is this?" I whispered, walking over to the bathroom door. I could hear the shower running and Andrew singing at the top of his lungs.

"An old friend," the unknown caller said.

I knew it was a lie. Of all the men I'd known in my past—and there were many—none of them would consider themselves my friend. "What do you want?" I demanded.

"Is that any way to greet an old friend?" He laughed.

"How do you know me?" I was struggling to calm

my breathing, hoping my heart rate would follow suit, but it didn't.

"Oh, we go way back," he said, "back before you became Andrew Carlton's arm candy. You know…back before you got that bling on your finger."

I stared at the eight-carat creation sitting on my ring finger. The pink diamond was a symbol of Andrew's love and devotion to me, but if this person really knew me and had something against me, I knew 'the bling', Andrew, and everything we shared could be gone in the twinkling of an eye.

I took a deep, cleansing breath and exhaled. Walking slowly across the carpeted floor, I tried to process my rambling thoughts. I didn't recognize the voice, but considering it had been nearly nine years since I had wreaked havoc on so many lives, that was to be expected.

"What do you want?" I asked again, more sternly this time.

"That's pretty simple," he said. "I want you, Tatiana."

I was so caught up in trying to figure out who was on the other end of the phone that I didn't hear the shower cut off or Andrew re-enter the room.

"Babe, who is it?" He stood at the edge of our king-sized bed with a thick towel wrapped around his waist. His chest was still glistening with tiny drops of water.

"Aww. Is that hubby-to-be?" the voice on the other end of the receiver asked. "Why don't you let me speak to him?"

"No!" I answered quickly.

"No what?" Andrew stood across the room staring at me.

"Um, not you, boo," I said, trying to get my nerves under control. "It's some damn telemarketer trying to sell me something," I lied.

"Just hang up," Andrew said casually.

I watched as he dried the rest of his body off then began smoothing shea butter over his muscles.

"Don't worry, Tatiana," the man taunted. "Your secret's safe with me."

I exhaled softly.

"At least for now," he added sarcastically.

Click.

Before I could respond, the line went dead, and I just stood there stunned, holding the phone in my hand. *Who was that? How did he get our number?*

"What were they selling?" Andrew stood in his boxers, stepping into a pair of jeans.

"Um, magazines," I said nervously.

He stared at me attentively.

Get it together, Essence. Listening to my inner voice, I forced my biggest smile. "Oh, I didn't want to be rude, so I let him talk," I explained. "You know most of them are just college kids trying to make a buck."

"That was sweet of you." He smiled at me sweetly.

"I try," I said with a shrug. I moved slowly back across the room to the nightstand. My hand shook uncontrollably as I placed the phone back in its cradle.

"Baby, are you okay?" His voice was full of concern as he watched me.

"Um, yeah." I smiled again. "I'm fine—just a little hungry." I watched as he slipped a wife beater over his head and then a loose-fitting Atlanta Fire t-shirt.

"I can stay here if you need me," he said, pulling me into his arms. "We can have breakfast together. We can lie around and play house before we go out to tonight," he continued, stroking my bare back.

"Tonight?"

"Did you forget already?" he asked, staring at me. "The party?" he reminded me.

I was so lost in my thoughts that I had forgotten about our engagement party. "Oh, yeah. I completely forgot," I admitted, slightly embarrassed.

"Are you feeling okay? Are you sure you don't want me to stay here this morning?"

Wrapping my arms around his waist, I closed my eyes. I turned my head so my cheek rested against his chest. "No, you go ahead." I wanted to accept his offer, but I knew I would be distracted because of the mysterious call. I didn't want Andrew worrying—or more importantly, prying into my strange behavior. Something inside of me was telling me things were about to get messy. That same ominous something was also telling me this was the calm before my storm.

Chapter 2

(Natalie)

I stood in my living room with a thousand thoughts running through my head and my hormones on high alert. I needed sexual gratification, and I needed it right then and now. Some women eat when they're stressed, and others like to shop, but me? I fuck, plain and simple. In my mind, there is no better stress reliever than making a bed rock while busting a nut.

Pacing back and forth across the living room floor, I rubbed my hands across my naked breast. My nipples felt hot to the touch and grew warmer and tauter as I pulled and kneaded them softly. Underneath the massaging and rubbing of my hands, my chocolate peaks grew until they were painfully hard.

Inside my boy-shorts panties, my kitty throbbed intensely. The pleasure spot in between my thighs felt like it was slowly beginning to ignite. I wanted to slip my hand down behind the tiny elastic band and extinguish the flame, but I knew the relief would only be temporary, and my orgasm would only lead to an inferno. I needed to feel a man—a living, breathing man with a rock hard dick.

"I can't take this!" I screamed. The sound of my own desperate voice bounced through the lonely room and echoed off of the furnishings. My living room was empty, with the exception of a black leather sofa and a nicely polished brass stripper pole. The pole ran from the vaulted ceiling down to the hardwood floor. I had the pole installed when I purchased my town home, and I planned to use it for exercise. I come from good genes, but working out on a regular basis is definitely mandatory. If I hadn't been on my best behavior since moving to Atlanta, the pole would have also been used for private entertainment. I like to swing upside down from time and time, and I honestly do enjoy having an audience occasionally.

I suddenly came to the realization that I had no connects in Atlanta. In fact, I hadn't so much as taken another man's number! I had to remain incognito. I couldn't risk anyone running back to Andrew or the tabloids with dirty love stories involving his woman.

I continued to pace back and forth until the purring

in my panties could no longer be ignored. I stopped my stride abruptly and then ran up the winding staircase to my bedroom, right to the closet. Pushing the French doors open, I found exactly what I needed on the wire shelf. I quickly grabbed the handles of one of several plastic totes where I kept my goodies hidden. I pulled the tote down to the carpeted floor and plopped down next to it. I removed the plastic lid and laid it on the floor next to me. Rummaging through the collection of wigs, I found one of my favorites: auburn-red, silky-straight, and long enough to hang just past my shoulders. I called the piece Natalie because that was the alias I used whenever I wore it. Smiling, I stood, carrying Natalie with me.

My bathroom was equipped with a built-in vanity right next to the marble sink. The vanity had a mirror, bench, and six separate sliding drawers. I plopped down on the cushioned bench and pulled out the two top left drawers. In the first drawer, I stored a variety of makeup and concealers. In the second drawer were over a hundred pairs of Acuvue one-day contact lenses in a rainbow of colors. I selected my last pair of green lenses and made a mental note to pick up another box the next chance I got. Remaining undercover was a fulltime job in itself. I couldn't wait for the day to arrive when I could be free to be me.

After securing my hair underneath a snug stocking

cap, I affixed the wig on my head. I fluffed the straight-edge bang so it framed my forehead perfectly and then brushed the ends of the locks. I wasn't in the mood to apply a full face of makeup, so I opted for a layer of fire red lip gloss instead. After inserting the contact lens, I stared in the mirror, looking at my creation. The wig and the contacts gave me a completely different look, one I was extremely satisfied with. I slipped on my body-hugging red Ed Hardy dress and stepped into a pair of red open-toed leather three-inch heels. The dress barely covered my ass, and I loved it. I grabbed my matching Ed Hardy bag, snatched three crisp one-hundred-dollar bills out of the stash I kept hidden under my bed, and bounced down the stairs and out the front door.

I climbed into my 2009 red Dodge Charger SXT and pulled out of my driveway to head for the highway. Through my amped-up speakers, Robin Thicke crooned about providing sex therapy. I relaxed against the leather seat, allowing my mind and body to enter full prowl mode. I was a woman on a mission. It was only a little after noon, far too early for me to hit up a restaurant bar, but I knew there would be men everywhere, many on their lunch breaks, eager to satisfy a variety of hungers. This gave me unlimited potential to find a quality friend to satisfy my sexual appetite for the next couple of hours. I pulled onto I-75, merging with the flow of traffic. I wished I had my Aston Martin to push, but I would be riding in style soon enough. Patience is a virtue, one I had learned throughout the years.

Even in speeding traffic, I managed to turn heads. I smiled and occasionally blew a kiss to the passersby, who felt the desire to slow down and ride alongside of me. All of them were cute enough to flirt with, but none of them appeared sex worthy. Granted, I was only looking for a one-time lover, but I still had certain standards to live by, and a brother pushing a Toyota Corolla was not going to be able to keep up with them. I slowed down long enough to make my exit and then sped toward Copeland's Cheesecake Bistro. I pulled into the parking lot and secured a space.

I spotted my prey before I had the opportunity to kill the engine. He was exiting through the front doors. He had almond-colored skin, and he was wearing a dark suit and dark Gators. I guessed him to be about five-seven, around 200 pounds. He wore his hair in neat dreads that hung down to the top of his shoulders. I killed the engine and then reached over and removed a three-pack of condoms from the glove box; I'm an advocate for safe sex. I know my status, and I'm trying to keep it just the way it is: negative. I threw the Trojans in my bag and opened my door to step out of the car.

I watched as he stepped off the sidewalk into the

parking lot. He removed a set of keys from his pocket and disarmed an alarm. I was relieved that the alarm belonged to a blue Lexus Coupe, parked just one space down from where I was standing. There was nothing in between us but an empty space and opportunity.

I hit the locks on my door and closed the door, locking my keys inside. "Damn it!" I screamed. I banged my hand on the driver's side window lightly. In the reflection of the glass, I could see my prey was watching. Smiling to myself, I continued with my performance. "Please open!" I whined, pulling on the door handle. I ran around to the passenger door and tried to pull on the handle, knowing it would do no good. "Shit!" I yelled. I walked back around the car and leaned against the driver's side door. I lowered my head, just to add dramatic effect. *Playing the damsel in distress always gets 'em*, I thought to myself.

"Excuse me," he spoke with a deep accent.

I raised my head slowly, pretending to dab at imaginary tears. When I looked in his eyes, I wanted to throw my legs around his waist! His eyes were the color of the ocean, a deep, breathtaking blue. His skin was clear and hairless and begged to be touched. It took every ounce of my being to suppress a smile as I grumbled, "Yes?"

"Do you need some help?"

I stared at his lips. They were thin but smooth. I

imagined the pleasure I was going to receive from them. Just thinking about it made my legs tremble. "I locked my keys in my car," I said, sniffing. "I don't know how I could be so stupid."

His eyes dropped from mine to my breasts and then back up again. "It can happen to anyone." He smiled.

Lord, he has some pretty teeth! So far, the brother was batting a thousand. The only thing that could put him out of the game would be a little dick or being gay. Judging by the way he was scanning my body with his eyes, I didn't have to worry about the latter. "Well, it happened to me," I said depressingly. I dropped my head again.

He reached out and lifted my chin with his hand. Not only was the man super sexy, but he smelled delicious! His scent was masculine but not too heavy. "I have roadside assistance." He smiled. "We can call a locksmith."

It wasn't the car door I needed a locksmith for; I needed someone to unlock the orgasm I had bolted up inside of me about to burst its way out! "Thank you," I said, sweetly touching his hand. I massaged his wrist softly. "But my hotel is not far. I can walk."

He held his hand in place on my chin, allowing me to continue rubbing his wrist. "No, let me give you a ride."

Oh, you're gonna give me a ride alright, I thought. "I don't want to inconvenience you," I sighed and lowered my eyes, giving him a seductive look.

"I can't let you walk," he said with a brilliant smile. "I would never forgive myself if something happened to you." Lowering his hand from my chin, he stepped back. "So, what do you say?" he asked.

"Can I give you a ride?" He wasn't smiling any longer. In fact, there was something very suggestive about the way he stated the question. When I ran my tongue nonchalantly across my bottom lip, his eyes grew wide with excitement.

"You most certainly can." I smiled. I watched him as he walked over to the Lexus and held open the passenger door. *Such a gentleman! Let's hope he's a freak too!* I sashayed my way over to the car and climbed in. My dress slid up my thighs, leaving very little to the imagination. He scanned the length of my legs with his eyes and smiled brightly. I wondered what he was thinking. As he shut the door, I reminded myself he was a man and I was a very sexy woman. There was no doubt in my mind he, too, was thinking about sex.

He climbed behind the wheel, shut the door, and started the engine. "Which hotel are you staying at?" he asked, sliding the gear shift into drive.

"What's close by?" I asked, shifting in the leather seat. I positioned my body so I was leaning on the center console.

He looked confused. "There're a couple in the area, but I thought you said you were staying at one in particular?"

Reaching over him, I ran my hand across his thigh. He looked surprised but not disappointed. I worked my fingers up his thigh to his crotch. To my delight, I found something definitely worth my while lodged snugly beneath the material. "Let's go to whichever one you like," I said, tugging on his zipper.

He grabbed my wrist, stopping me. "Why?" he asked, his blue eyes locked on me.

"To say thank you." I smiled, reaching up to caress his dreads. "You know…for being such a gentleman."

He quickly shifted back into park. "I've been a gentleman all my life," he said seriously, "but the only women who have just thrown their panties at me have all wanted something in return."

I could not believe my luck. He actually wanted to rationalize my behavior! Granted, had he met me years earlier, I would have had a hidden agenda, but these days, I wanted exactly what I was offering—nothing more and nothing less. "I don't want anything," I reassured him.

He looked like he was contemplating what decision to make.

"Well, I do want something," I added, again attempting to unzip his pants.

He grabbed my wrist and frowned. "Dedra put you

up to this shit!“ he snapped.

Who the hell is Dedra? I thought, staring at him.

“Yeah, this bullshit got her name written all over it! You tell that triflin’ ho’ I ain’t paying her a damn dime!” he rambled, hitting the steering wheel with his fist. “She wants half my moneyand all she did was lay on her back! My mama warned me about that bitch!” he yelled.

“Look, Dedra didn‘t put me up to anything,” I snapped. “I don’t even know a Dedra!”

“Then what is this about?” he asked. He was breathing so hard he was practically fuming at the mouth.

“I’m just trying to get with you,” I said. “Nothing more, nothing less.”

I reached out to find his zipper again. This time, he didn’t move my hand. I reached in between the material, past the opening of his boxers, and found what I was looking for. I pulled out my new friend and began to stroke it slowly. He closed his eyes and then relaxed against the driver’s seat. I teased him with a hand job until his joystick was fully ready for play.

He opened his eyes and looked at me. “I have to get back to the office.” He exhaled. “Maybe we should get together later.”

What the hell?! First Dedra, and now it’s his damn job! There was no way I was going to give him a rain check. It was either now or never. He had already wasted enough of my time. *Maybe he is gay* "Tell them you'll be late," I whispered before pressing my lips to his. At first, I could sense his resistance, and then, without another word, he parted his lips, allowing his warm tongue to make contact with mine. I allowed him to have control of the kiss, and I followed his slow, sensual rhythm. You can tell a lot about a man by the way he kisses, and from the way he was taking his time, I assumed him to be a gentle and attentive lover.

I moved my lips from his down to his earlobe. I pulled and then sucked on his lobe hungrily. "I'm ready to go," I whispered, "unless you want to do this right here." I pulled back and relaxed in my seat.

He looked at me, shook his head, and smiled before putting the car in drive and pulling out of the parking lot. "I need to stop for rubbers," he said quickly.

"I already have some." I reached into my bag and pulled out my three pack. Dangling them in the air, I winked my eye at him.

He nodded and threw me a slightly strained smile. "Can I at least have your name?" he asked as he pulled onto the interstate.

"My name is Natalie," I lied, while looking out the window, "but for now, I'll be whoever you want me to be."

"Natalie works for me." He laughed. "And you can

call me Malcolm."

I didn't know nor did I care if he had given me his birth name. I planned to call him whatever I pleased.

* * * * *

Fifteen minutes later, the two of us were at the Holiday Inn. I slid the electronic key card in the slot to open the door. I walked in with Malcolm following close behind. Looking around the room, I observed that it appeared clean. There were a small desk and chair, two nightstands, a dresser with mirror, a twenty-seven-inch TV, and a cozy-looking recliner. I didn't care about any of those things, though, all I needed was the nice king-sized bed. I walked over to the nightstand, sat my bag down, and took a seat on the corner of the bed. Malcolm shut the door and secured the additional safety latch.

"Are you nervous?" I teased.

"Naw," he said, watching me carefully. He stood by the door looking unbelievably tense.

It was obvious if the two of us were going to get the party started, I was going to have to be the DJ. I kicked my heels off and slid back on the bed, against the headboard. I spread my legs wide, exposing my hairless pussycat. I could tell by his expression that he was pleased. I watched as he carefully removed his jacket and laid it on the small cushioned chair. I was geared up and prepared to watch him strip down to nothing for me, but after removing his jacket, he just walked over and sat down in the recliner. *I guess if I want something done, I'm going to have to do it myself,* I thought with a sigh.

I climbed off the bed and walked over to where he was sitting. Slowly, I lifted my dress up and over my head. I dropped the dress to the floor and stood in front of him wearing nothing but my birthday suit.

His eyes traveled from my face down to my French pedicure and then back up again.

"You like?" I asked, turning around slowly for him to inspect me from all angles.

"Hell yeah." He reached out and pulled me to him. Whatever guard he previously had up was now gone. Grabbing my breasts with both hands, he took his time licking and sucking each of my nipples.

I grabbed his head, pulling him closer. I wanted him to open wide, to get as much of my titties as he possibly could in his warm, wet mouth. "Yes," I moaned. I spread my legs and guided his right hand right to my hot spot. His hands were smooth, but strong, and at first, he grabbed my pussy hard.

"Damn, your pussy is phat," he moaned before spreading my lips and easing his finger inside. He moved slowly in and out.

I felt his hand move, and then another finger and

another, until there were three pushing inside of me. I rotated my hips slowly, grinding on his hand. His fingers felt good, but not good enough. I needed the real thing. "Stand up," I ordered.

He removed his mouth and hands from me, and I took a step back, allowing him room to stand. Once he was on his feet, I dropped to my knees. I moved quickly, unbuttoning his pants and pulling them, along with his paisley boxers, down to his ankles. His pole stood at full attention. I looked up, staring into his eyes while I wrapped my lips around the head of his thick dick. I sucked on his head slowly, rolling my tongue back and forth.

"Damn," he moaned.

I pulled his head from my lips and then licked up and down his shaft until it was slippery wet. Once I had licked every inch of his dick, I opened my mouth wide and deep throated him.

"Shit!" he half screamed, closing his eyes.

I could sense he was close to erupting, and the last thing I wanted was to push him over the edge before I got mine. I reached over onto the nightstand into my purse and removed the condoms. I handed one to him and waited patiently as he removed his shirt and tie, revealing nicely toned biceps and a hard six pack. Once he had our protection safely in place, I jumped up, wrapping my legs around his waist. I kissed him hard on the mouth, sucking and pulling on his bottom lip.

Holding me tightly, Malcolm eased me down onto the bed. When he entered me, I swear his dick felt like ice cream on an Alabama summer's day: refreshing. He moved slow and easy, rotating and grinding his hips.

I wrapped my legs around his waist tighter, holding him in a grip that could choke a python.

"You feel so good," he moaned, kissing me softly on the lips.

"So do you."

He licked his way down my neck, stopping at my breasts. I watched as he used his tongue to trace wet circles around my areola. He started with the left and then licked his way to the right one. Inside my pussy, his stroke became stronger with every rotation. He pushed deeper and deeper with every move.

"Oh…" I moaned with pleasure. It felt like liquid lava was coursing through my veins, and I was on the verge of an orgasmic eruption. "Harder," I pleaded.

Malcolm stared at me passionately. The heat in his eyes was erotic and exhilarating. Pushing my legs up and out until I was in a full split, he pulled his knees up and planted one foot firmly on the bed. Our new position allowed him to feed me all ten inches of his magic stick. "Mmm," he grunted, moving in and out of my wet kitty.

His breathing was deep and heavy as his balls slapped roughly against my ass.

"Just like that!" I squealed.

Malcolm pushed in and out, in and out, and it wasn't long before I felt that special tingle in the pit of my stomach. My body began to tense up, and my legs began to shake. I wanted to cum and cumming was exactly what I did. I was speechless as one orgasm followed by another rippled through my body.

Malcolm began to pound harder until he, too, was cumming. His body tensed up as hot sweat dripped off his muscles and onto my face. "Shit," he grunted before he collapsed onto the bed next to me. "That was…" He breathed heavily. "Damn," he panted.

I rolled onto my side and playfully kissed his neck. "It was good?" I asked.

"Hell yeah." He looked at me with a look that screamed *"I want some more."* It was a look I'd seen many times before.

"You never called the office," I said, rolling over off the bed, trying to remind him we both had things to do.

"I *am* the office," he said with a sly, proud grin. I watched as he reached over onto the floor and pulled a card from his pants. "Here," he said.

I walked over to the side of the bed and took his business card from him. His name really was

Malcolm—Malcolm Drake, to be exact—and he was a senior partner for Drake & Associates, Attorneys at Law.

I shook my head laughing lightly. "This explains why you were so paranoid." I laughed.

"Partly," he said.

"So who is this Dedra?" I asked.

He shook his head, exhaling loudly. "My wife," he said. "Hopefully, my soon-to-be ex-wife."

"Messy divorce?"

"Messy aint the word for it." He frowned. "That tramp is ruthless."

"Let me guess," I said, pausing shortly. "She's a gold digger?"

"That, and a liar."

"Take it from me," I said sincerely, "things will work out for the best. It doesn't pay to do good people wrong." I scooped my dress up off the floor and headed toward the bathroom. I needed to shower and call a cab right away. I had an event to attend and could not be late.

"In a hurry?" he asked, sitting up on the edge of the bed.

"Sorta," I said, looking over my shoulder at him.

"Do you need a ride?"

"No. I'll call a cab," I said, giving him a sweet smile.

"What about your car?"

"I have a spare key in my purse," I confessed with a wink.

"Wow." He laughed, shaking his head. "So you played me?"

Played was such a strong word considering the pleasure the two of us had just shared. I considered both of us winners. I turned to look him directly in his eyes, but his expression was unreadable. I couldn't tell if he was upset or not, but frankly, I didn't care. "No, boo." I smiled. "I just saw something I wanted and went after it, that's all."

"Are you sure you're not a lawyer too? You'd make a damn good one with that kind of attitude."

"Nope," I chuckled, "but you never know when I'll need a *good* lawyer."

Chapter 3

(Essence)

Andrew and I entered the banquet room of the Omni at the CNN Center for the engagement party Simone had graciously offered to throw for us. Andrew wore a simple black Armani tux, while I wore a red silk gown that stopped just above my knees. The dress was strapless with a diamond-shaped cutout that dipped dangerously low in the back. My red stilettos made my legs appear much longer than they actually are. I wore my hair down in a cascade of soft curls. With the exception of my engagement ring and a pair of one-carat diamond studs, I wore no jewelry. I liked to keep my accessories simple.

The room was decorated with mini white lights, arches made with black and white balloons, and round tables covered with black linen cloths. On each table sat a trio of glass votive holders with white candles. Around the votive holders were single strings of white lights. Simone kept with her black and white theme by adding folding white wooden chairs to each table. A dance floor had been brought in that stretched from the back of the room up the left side. The floor was busy with people chitchatting and sipping on drinks. All the women wore evening gowns or party dresses, and all the men—servers included—wore tuxedos. Security was fully enforced, and to my delight, the paparazzi had been excluded. Andrew made Simone vow that our special evening would not be turned into a media circus, and it appeared she managed to keep her promise. I scanned the room, noticing Andrew's teammates and business colleagues were all present. I also noticed a few other famous faces were in attendance.

"It's about time." Simone seemed to appear out of nowhere. She wore an elegant one-shoulder, ice-blue evening gown that touched her ankles. The material hung loosely on her thin frame. Her hair was pulled up on top of her head in a neat bun.

I made a mental note to one day offer to design a gown that would properly complement her wafer-thin body. I figured the day would eventually come where the two of us were cordial enough that I could offer her a makeover, and trust me, she could have used one. It wasn't that Simone was unattractive. She had clear, light skin with dark brown eyes, an oval-shaped face, and full lips. She was actually pretty, but she had no idea what to do with it. I'm sure she saw herself as conservative, but the way she dressed did nothing for her image.

"Better late than never," Andrew said, giving her a small smile.

"Andrew, you're three hours late!" She was obviously frustrated. "All the guest have arrived."

"Good. You can let them know the guests of honor are here now." He patted her on the shoulder and then led me by the hand onto the crowded floor. I didn't bother looking over my shoulder to see her reaction.

"Drew!" Carlito yelled, pushing his way toward us. He greeted Andrew with a brotherly hug and then kissed my cheek. "Wow!" he said before he let out a low whistle, scanning me with his eyes.

I smiled.

"You definitely have the baddest chick in the room," he said to Andrew.

Slipping his arm around my waist, Andrew smiled like a kid who had just won a prize at the county fair. "Tell me something I don't know."

"And is this one of the designs Andrew has been bragging about?" Carlito asked, looking at my dress.

I smiled proudly and nodded. The gown was from

my own personal collection. When I first moved to Atlanta, my main goal was to attend the Atlanta School of Arts. After a year of schooling, I decided to drop out—not because I was no longer interested in design, as I'd always had a flare for fashion, but because I couldn't stand the thought of being confined to a classroom. I wanted to be out in the workforce attempting to make a name for myself.

I also knew the time would come when the money I had stashed away over the years would run out, and I would have to have a backup plan. I wanted that backup plan to be legitimate, and with my spending habits, I knew my stash would run out far before I got a degree. So, I continued to work and improve my fashion skills.

"I can't wait to see your designs on the runways." Carlito grinned, looking at Andrew.

Andrew nodded his head, smiling in return.

"Someday, I hope." I smiled. The dream of being a well-known designer was one I desperately wanted to fulfill, but you have to crawl before you can walk. However, considering I had yet to secure buyers for my creations, I wasn't even in the crawling stage yet.

"I know my baby is going to do great things someday." Andrew grinned, looping his fingers through mine.

"If you ask me, she's already done a great thing," Simone said, stepping up behind the three of us. She stepped around Andrew and me to stand next to Carlito. "I mean, she managed to snag one of Atlanta's most sought-after bachelors and the League's most talented players." There was a hint of sarcasm in her voice. I wondered if I was the only person who picked up on it.

"Yes, I'm a lucky girl," I said, staring her in her eyes, "envied by many."

Simone frowned at me, showing her obvious disapproval with my sarcasm.

"I think Andrew hit the jackpot," Carlito chimed in. "I mean, when I think about the hood rats that were jocking him before Essence came along…" Carlito chuckled, looking at Simone from head to toe. "Eww! My boy lucked out!" Carlito laughed.

Andrew smiled, laughing along with him. Simone's face turned an unflattering shade of red. It was obvious Carlito, too, had picked up on Simone's underlying jealousy. "I consider myself a very lucky man." Andrew pulled me into his arms and kissed me.

At that moment, it was if we were the only two people in the room. I wrapped my arms around his strong neck, allowing his lips to take control of mine. Our tongues touched, teased, and rubbed each other exotically. I felt a warming sensation in the pit of my stomach. Pulling away, I tried hard to calm my breathing. I knew if we kept going, the two of us would be upstairs in a room, making the bed rock.

"Well…" said Simone, looking embarrassed as well as slightly disgusted from our public display of affection. "Now that the two of you have given your guests an eyeful, maybe you can make your rounds around the room and thank them for coming." She turned on her tacky heels and strutted off.

"That girl needs to get laid." Carlito chuckled.

I nodded my head in agreement.

"Hey, she's single and you're single, so—"

"Don't even think about it!" Carlito cut Andrew off. "I'm here to have a good time, not to do charity work."

"I'm just sayin'."

"I know what you're just sayin', and I'm sayin' hell no."

I watched the two of them go back and forth over their friendly debate about Simone until the sound of Andrew's cell phone ringing brought their conversation to an abrupt end.

"I'll catch up with you two later." Carlito gave Andrew a pat on the back and then worked his way back through the crowd.

Andrew reached in to his jacket to retrieve his Blackberry. He glanced at the screen for a second and then answered. "This is Andrew." He looked at me and smiled as he was talking to whoever-it-was. "Okay.

That‘s great. She‘s right here."

"Who is it?" I whispered curiously.

"Someone interested in buying your designs." Andrew smiled and handed me the phone.

"Take a number. I'll call them back." Although I was ecstatic about the call, I didn't want to discuss business at our special party. I had made Andrew vow that no business would be discussed at the party, and I couldn't ask him to keep a promise I was willing to break myself.

"Baby, there is no way in hell I'm going to let you miss this possible opportunity," he said, handing me the phone. "This might be what you've been waiting for. Take the call, Essence."

In that instant, I swear I loved him more than I had five minutes earlier. I took the phone from his hand while mouthing; "I love you." I held the phone up to my ear. "This is Essence," I said, excited about the possible opportunity on the other end.

"See how easy it is for me to find you?"

My stomach clenched from the sound of his voice. "Yes," I said nervously. Andrew's beautiful eyes were locked on me, and I could feel the perspiration gathering on my skin. "I'm sorry, but how did you get this number?" I asked, trying to sound normal and professional.

"No matter where you are, I *can* find you," he said

confidently. "I think I just proved that."

"Oh, it's not a problem," I stuttered. "I just prefer to use my number for business."

"I'll try to keep that in mind." He laughed.

My flesh felt like it was crawling. "Baby, I'm going to step out of the room for a second," I told Andrew, while covering the phone with my hand.

"Sure, babe." He leaned in and kissed my cheek. "I'll be here when you get back."

I quickly pushed my way through the crowd, smiling and nodding at guests as I went. I passed a beautiful caramel-skinned sister with long platinum hair. She nodded her head at me and winked her eye. I smiled in returned. There was something familiar about the woman, but at that moment, I didn't have time to try and place a name with the face.

"Who are you?" I whispered into the phone through clenched teeth. I made my way out into the hall and slipped out the side door of the hotel. To my relief, I was alone as I stood on the side of the building.

"It doesn't matter who I am," he said. "What's important is that I know who you are."

"And who exactly do you think I am?" I kept my voice low.

"I know who you are," he said. "Tatiana Sledge…a lying-ass slut."

And then there was silence.

I could feel the onset of a headache as I paced back and forth along the side of the hotel. I took a deep breath through my nose and exhaled softy through my lips. "How much do you want?" I finally asked.

"How much?"

"Yes," I said. "Name your price."

"Oh, Tatiana," he laughed. His laugh was really starting to get to me. It was sick and twisted and so condescending. The sooner I had the man and his twisted sense of humor out of my life, the better. "This isn't about money," he said. "This is all about you," he continued. "I told you all I want is you."

"*Why* do you want *me*?" I asked.

"Because," he said, "you're the best."

"Enjoy your party," he said. "I'll be in touch."

"You know my number," I said. "Don't call this one again. Leave Andrew out of this."

"As you wish," he said quickly before the call ended.

"Leave Andrew out of what?"

I turned quickly on my heels, only to see Simone standing by the exit door. She stood with her bony arms crossed across her breasts. Ignoring her questioning glare, I walked toward her. I was not in the mood to deal with her. "How long have you been eavesdropping on me?" I asked, attempting to step around her.

She placed her hand against the exit door, stopping me from grabbing the door handle. "I came to look for you."

I said nothing and just stared at her.

"To see why you left Andrew alone to greet your guests," she said with attitude.

"I had a business call," I said, trying hard to maintain my composure. "Andrew was aware, and he said it was fine if I took the call outside."

"You never answered my question," she said, looking at me suspiciously.

"What?" I was growing impatient with her.

"What are you trying to leave Andrew out of?"

"The person on the phone wants to purchase my designs," I lied. "But they wanted to include Andrew in their advertising."

"For dresses?" she frowned. "Why would they want Andrew to sell dresses?"

"Well, he is the League's most talented player," I said, mocking her earlier comment.

She cut her eyes at me then stepped back so I could open the door. "If I were you, I'd be very careful who I associate with," she said, folding her arms across her thin chest. "I'd hate for someone or something to pop up that could tarnish Andrew's image."

I grabbed the door handle and jerked the door open.

"Yeah, I'm sure that's the problem," I said, stepping through the open door.

"What's the problem?" she asked.

"You're not me," I said bluntly before shutting the door in her face. On a normal day, I would have handled Simone's nosiness with more class, but this wasn't the normal occasion. I had too many thoughts running through my mind. I had to find out who the man was. At the moment, he had the upper hand. He knew who I was and how to contact me. I needed to turn the tables and quickly. I had learned a long time ago that giving someone else the upper hand is a quick way to cut your own throat.

* * * * *

I returned to the ballroom to find Andrew sitting at table with Carlito and a beautiful olive-skinned female, who I recognized as one of the women from Cycle 3 of *America's Next Top Model*. They seemed to be getting along quite well, laughing and whispering like two high school sweethearts.

"How did it go?" Andrew asked, pulling out my chair for me.

"Oh, it went well," I lied. "The two of us are going to get together soon to discuss business."

His eyes shone proudly. "That's wonderful, baby!" He

kissed my cheek softly. "Oh, I almost forgot. Someone left you a gift," he said, reaching into his jacket pocket. He slid the shiny gift box over to me. There was a small silver gift tag with my name on it attached to the box.

"Who is it from?" I asked, while opening the small square box.

"I'm not sure," Andrew said. "It was sitting on our table when we came over."

Inside the box was a small hourglass with a note. "Your time is almost up," Andrew read aloud, looking at the note. "Cute," he said, laughing. "They're trying to warn you your days as a single lady are almost over."

"Yeah," I said, faking a smile. I agreed with Andrew, but deep inside I knew the note meant so much more, and it wasn't cute at all.

Chapter 4

(Essence)

Spring training for the Atlanta Fire meant Andrew's mornings and afternoons were now filled with intense practicing, and his regular season and additional travelling was on the way. However, I didn't mind. I had my clothing line to work on, as well as my volunteer activities. Andrew was more than happy for me to be a homemaker, but I needed my own career and my own causes. The thought of sitting around the house all the time made me nauseous. I needed more excitement in my day than just washing my man's dirty drawers.

I was determined not to let the mysterious phone calls I had been receiving stop me from doing the things I loved. I figured if whoever-it-was wanted to put me on blast, they would have already done so. I knew it was a mind game to them and half of their pleasure came from making me sweat and suffer. I was once the queen of mind games; they would have to come harder with it to stop my stride.

Once a week, I volunteered to work with the residents at the Lenbrook Retirement Community in Buckhead. Until I started working with the residents, I had the ill-conceived notion that retirement communities were just high-priced apartments with a bunch of sad elderly people waiting to take their last breath. Lenbrook was far from that. The residents there were full of life, living their lives to the fullest. From weightlifting to Tai Chi and dancing, there was always something to do. I was amazed at their energy, and sometimes I even had trouble keeping up with them.

One resident in particular had become my favorite, a petite widower by the name of Ethel. Ethel was a sassy, sexy woman with very few wrinkles on her mocha-colored skin and a well-toned body. Ethel was a fashionista who stayed on top of the latest trends and the hottest gossip. She actually helped me when it came to sewing and putting together my designs, a hobby she very much enjoyed.

On Ethel's sixtieth birthday, the residents and I threw her a party. For the celebration, I hired a professional party planner to decorate the resident clubhouse to resemble a fifties-style diner, to coordinate with the theme the staff and I selected. There were pink and white balloons and vinyl records hanging from the ceiling, pink tablecloths that resembled poodle skirts, and a jukebox spinning old-school tunes off of authentic record albums. After we danced and enjoyed a game of charades, we all gathered around the glowing birthday girl as she opened her presents.

"Wow!" Ethel said, holding up what looked like an extremely long animal print scarf. "Thanks, Carol."

"You're welcome." Carol smiled brightly.

"Carol?" Ethel asked, looking at the gift with raised eyebrows.

"Yes?"

"What is it?" Ethel questioned.

"Ethel, it's a scarf," I whispered.

"No, it's one of those head wraps," Mr. Johnson, one of the residents, jumped in, pushing his glasses up on his nose.

"It's a belt," Carol snapped, rolling her eyes at me. Carol was one of Ethel's closest friends and just as feisty. I nicknamed them Thelma and Louise, even though Ethel was black and Carol was Irish.

"What kind of belt?" Ethel asked, standing and wrapping the creation around her waist. It took six rotations before she could actually tie the thing securely.

"I saw one on QVC. The new in-thing is wide belts

that hang at the waist," Carol said proudly. "So I made you one."

"Carol, you can't sew," Ethel reminded her.

"Yes, but I told you I was thinking of making sewing my new hobby."

"And you had to wait 'til my birthday to give it a go?" Ethel questioned.

"As a friend, I thought you would appreciate the gesture," Carol said, crossing her arms across her breasts.

"I would have appreciated you going over to Lennox more!" Ethel replied.

"It's the thought that counts!"

"Tomorrow do you *think* you can go down and get me a real present?"

"What I *think* is you can kiss my a—"

"Ladies! " Mr. Johnson interrupted, putting his arm around both of the women. "Is that any way for friends to carry on?" I watched Mr. Johnson as he got his feel on, on the sly, rubbing his hands up and down the women's shoulders and backs.

"Did we ask you?" Ethel asked, knocking the man's hand off her shoulder.

"When we want your opinion, we'll let you know," Carol added.

I watched as she swatted Mr. Johnson's arm off her shoulder, and I shook my head, laughing slightly as the two of them went back and forth at the poor man. "I'll be right back!" I yelled before stepping away to answer my cell phone. "Hello."

"Did you miss me?"

The sound of the man's voice immediately pissed me off. "How long do you plan on doing this?" I asked through clenched teeth.

"Who knows?" He laughed. " A year? Two? Maybe six? However long it takes."

"You need to get a life," I snapped.

"I had a life until you entered it," he said.

"What happened?" I asked sarcastically. "Did I break your heart or something?"

"Yes, Tatiana. You did."

"Essence, I'm about to open your gifts!" Ethel yelled from the other side of the room, "and you better not have took the cheap route like Carol!"

"That's life," I said. "Man up."

"C'mon, Essence!" someone yelled.

"As much as I'm enjoying this, I have to go now," I said, before hanging up. I rejoined the party just in time to catch Ethel opening up my first gift.

"An iPod!" Ethel squealed. "It's just what I wanted. Now I can listen to Gucci while I'm on the treadmill," she said, blowing me a kiss.

"What's a Gucci?" Mr. Johnson whispered to Carol.

"Gucci Mane. He's an artist," Carol said, rolling her eyes. "You've never heard of Gucci?"

"Hell no," Mr. Johnson said, shaking his head.

"This is why I don't date old men," she said, sucking on her teeth.

I laughed. Pushing thoughts of the disturbing phone calls out of my head, I managed to slip back into party mode.

"I love it!" Ethel smiled after opening up her next present, the Louis Vuitton handbag I had purchased for her. "Thank you, sweetie."

"You're welcome." I smiled.

"One more, Ethel," Carol said, handing her a purple gift bag.

"Well hello," Ethel exclaimed with a grin.

I watched as she pulled out a leather corset and leather crotchless panties.

"Now that's what I'm talking bout!" Mr. Johnson said with a devious smile.

I watched as he and some of the other men present smiled and nodded there heads in agreement.

"Who is this from?" Ethel asked, reaching back into the bag. This time, she pulled out a small box and a DVD.

"It's from Essence," Carol said casually.

A few members of the staff looked at me like I had

lost my damn mind.

"What? No," I said quickly. "That's not from me."

"The bag has your name on it," Carol said, looking at me.

"These pearls are broken," Ethel said, holding up the string of beads she had pulled from the box.

My mouth dropped open when I saw that they weren't pearls, but instead anal beads. I could feel droplets of sweat developing on my forehead.

"Actually, it says it's *to* Essence," Monica, the activity manager, stated, looking more carefully at the gift tag. She smiled at me and handed me the tag. "I'm guessing Essence accidentally picked this bag up when she was grabbing your gifts, Ethel."

"Yes," I said, nodding my head quickly. "I'm sorry." The truth was, I had only entered the building with two boxes, which meant someone had left the bag there for me.

"It's okay," Monica whispered nudging me. "I know how racy wedding gifts can be."

"Yeah," I laughed lightly.

"Oh well," Ethel said, dropping the items back in the bag, "but you have got to get me one of these." She held up the corset.

"Sure I will." I smiled nervously.

* * * * *

I hurried into the family room and popped the DVD in the player. There wasn't a label on the disc, and my natural instinct was telling me that whatever was on it was for my eyes only. When the movie came on, I felt like I would pee in my g-string at any moment. As I half expected it would be, the movie was a homemade flick, and I was the star. I couldn't see the face of my co-star, but it was evident by his moans that he was enjoying the way I was riding and grinding on his stick. The camera was conveniently zoomed in on my back and my ass. My face was hidden from view, but I knew my voice and my own body, and the woman working it out on the bed was definitely me. "Yes…" I moaned on the disc. "Is it good, Daddy?"

I popped the disc out of the DVD player and smashed it with my heel, causing it to break into two pieces. I had done a lot of sexing in my life, and I didn't have the first clue which man it could be. I didn't remember ever making a sex tape, but it's a known fact that just because you don't know doesn't mean they don't exist. The thought of more tapes surfacing made me nervous. *What if there are others that actually reveal my identity?* Suddenly, my little problem with the phone stalker seemed a lot bigger.

* * * * *

Andrew arrived home that night and found me soaking in our luxurious outdoor hot tub. He looked tired, as he often did after training, but good nonetheless. "Hey, beautiful." He smiled, leaning down to kiss me on the forehead.

"Hey, baby."

"Room for two in there?" He smiled mischievously.

My hair hung loosely at my shoulders as I rose, revealing my birthday suit. "More than enough." I smiled at him invitingly and climbed onto the edge of the tub. He blinked, quickly admiring my frame. I reached up and wrapped my wet arms around his neck and kissed him slowly. His lips greeted mine eagerly. Slipping my tongue in his mouth, I traced the tip of his tongue with mine. His strong hands moved to the curve of my back and then down to my ample ass. Dropping my hands to his crotch, I kneaded and rubbed his erection with enough passion to ignite even the most stubborn fire.

"To what do I owe this?" he moaned.

I quickly unbuttoned the denim shorts he wore and pulled his thick joystick through the opening of his boxers. "Oh, nothing. I just missed you today." I only stretched the truth a little. The truth was, I always missed Andrew when he was gone, but now I was scared of what was going to come next from my stalker. I wrapped my lips around Andrew's thick head, sucking gently, while rolling my tongue slowly.

"That feels good," he whispered. He moved his hands to my hair, grabbing a handful of my locks.

I pulled back, kissing his head softly, and then plunged down on his dick swiftly. My actions caused him to jump and then moan loudly. I relaxed my throat, breathing in through my nose, allowing myself to deep throat his dick with ease. I worked Andrew's manhood thoroughly with my mouth until it began to weep. I released my grip on him and sat with my legs spread on the steps of the hot tub.

Andrew wasted no time entering me. His hands moved from my hair to my breasts and then to my ass. Our normal sex sessions were gentle and slow, but not this time. The two of us were straight fucking. Andrew pushed inside of my warm pussy as far as our bodies would allow him to go. The sound of the roaring hot tub was nothing compared to the sound of Andrew's sac slapping against my ass. Holding on to his thin t-shirt, I pulled him closer. Our lips and tongues attacked each other brutally. Andrew sucked on my tongue like it held the nectar of life. Clenching the muscles of my vagina tightly, I grabbed his rock hard dick.

"I love you," he moaned, burying his face in my neck.

"I love you." I felt a warm churning sensation inside of me. I wanted to fight the orgasm pushing its way to the surface, but Andrew felt too good. I wanted the pleasure to go on forever. "Andrew…" The moan escaped my lips while my body began to shake.

"I'm right here, baby." His stroke intensified as he penetrated deeper.

I closed my eyes and arched my back, allowing my liquid joy to flow freely. "Yessss," I slurred as my orgasm continued to shake my body.

Andrew kissed me softly, continuing to move in and out of my wet spot quickly. I felt his muscles tighten, and I knew he was approaching his peak. "Here it comes," he grunted heavily.

I wrapped my arms around his shoulders, relaxing as Andrew released his soldiers inside of me.

* * * * *

After our encounter on the hot tub, Andrew and I shared a long hot bath and then stretched out naked on top of our bed. I lay with my back to his chest, as he held me tightly in his arms. "Are you hungry?" I asked, stroking the fine hairs along his forearms gently.

"Nah, I'm good," he said, kissing me behind my ear. "Coach had a small buffet for us after practice."

"How did training go?"

"It was good," he said, laughing lightly. "Although it was nothing compared to the workout you just gave me."

"I just wanted to show you that you're the only man for me," I said honestly.

"Baby, I know that, and that's one of the reasons why I love you," he said, yawning. "From day one, you've been loyal, and you've kept it real with me."

I was glad I had my back to him. I knew if he saw the look in my eyes, he would know there was something I was keeping from him. I felt his chest rising and falling gently, followed by the low roaring of his snores. Closing my eyes, I exhaled softly. I was mentally exhausted. For the moment, I would put all my worries to the side. I would deal with them soon enough.

Chapter 5

(Marilyn)

I try to be good, but sometimes it feels like I'm allergic to good behavior, as if doing the right thing might cause my skin to swell into a hundred tiny little red, itchy blotches that not even a double dose of antibiotics could cure. I once heard someone say that what's in you will eventually come out of you, meaning, if it's in your nature to lie, you're going to lie; if it's in your nature to steal, you're going to steal; an if it's in your nature to be bad, you're going to be bad. So, when I left home to go do some innocent grocery shopping, I should have known my bad girl nature would kick in. I had on yet another one of my infamous disguises: a short-layered black wig, gray contacts, and a signature black mole drawn above my left lip. My attire was conservative for my taste but still ultra-sexy. I wore a pair of Seven jeans, black pumps, and a fitted black tank top with the words 'Spoil Me' embroidered in gold on the front. It was simple and sweet, but like I said, what's in you will come out of you.

I was minding my own business, dropping shiny Granny Smith apples in the plastic produce bag, when I saw him. He wore a pair of breakaway Nike athletic pants and a short-sleeved Nike t-shirt. The shirt was screaming to be let free from the mounds of muscles being held hostage by the fabric. I casually observed him as he gazed over a selection of mangos, kneading and caressing the fruit as if it were a woman's body. I dropped the last of four apples in the bag and then neatly twisted the end of the bag into a knot. I moved on to the grapes while the man continued to inspect the melons. *Hmm... is he really that into fruit or just plain lonely*? I wondered. Letting out a giggle, I shook my head, and that was all I needed to do to capture his attention. *Yep, he's lonely!* He raised his head, zooming his eyes in on me. I smiled victoriously as his dark brown eyes went from my face to my breasts and then down to my hips. I laughed again, and we stared at each other for a brief second. *Where have I seen him before?* His light-skinned baby face, low-cut deep waves, and pudgy nose looked familiar, but I couldn't put my finger on where I had seen him before. I chalked it up to déjà vu and moved in for the kill.

Swinging the handheld basket at my side, I stepped in his direction. "You do realize, more than two squeezes is considered foreplay," I teased.

Placing the mango back on the pile neatly, he laughed. "I have an obsession with good fruit *and* beautiful women," he said in a sultry, deep voice.

"You're acting like those mangos *are* women."

"Oh no," he said without cracking a smile, "trust me. I know a woman when I see and *feel* one."

I felt the sexual suggestion with every word he spoke, and I loved it. He may have had a baby face, but it was obvious I was dealing with a grown man. I shifted my weight from one leg to another and then placed my free hand on my hip. "You talk a big game for someone who likes to play cop a feel with fruit."

"I buy only the best." He laughed. Lowering his eyes seductively, he smiled at me.

"Too bad for you, I'm not for sale. " I smiled and blew him a kiss. Strolling off, I began a silent countdown in my head. *Ten... nine... eight... seven...*

"I didn't catch your name," he said, running up beside me.

"Maybe that's because I didn't throw it at you." I stepped in line at the express checkout, behind a plump redhead whose cart held far more than ten items. I rolled my eyes at her and began putting my items on the belt, right behind her Chunky Monkey ice cream. I could easily have bounced to the self-checkout line, but despite my frustration with the woman in front of me, I knew I was buying additional time with the sexy man.

"So, what's your name?" he asked, leaning in close to me.

"Why?" I pretended to be slightly annoyed.

"Well, because I'd like to get to know you better," he said, smiling.

"So you can grope me like those melons?" I asked, batting my eyes at him.

"Well, no," he said, laughing lightly.

"Too bad," I said seriously. "I would have taken you up on that one."

The redhead in front of me cleared her throat. I looked at the woman, and she frowned. *Oh no she didn't!* I cut my eyes at her, a subtle indication I was not seeking her approval. "Focus on your Chunky Monkey, sista," I whispered, in her direction.

"Well, I was thinking the two of us could at least have dinner first," he said, scanning my physique with his eyes. "From there, anything is possible."

My kitty jumped at the possibilities. "I'm Marilyn." I smiled, extending my hand to him.

"Nice to meet you, Marilyn." He took my hand and

kissed it softly. "I'm Deon."

"It's not good to pick up strangers," Big Red whispered to me while paying for her groceries.

I took my eyes from Deon long enough to lower them at her. "Who asked you?" I snapped.

She wiggled her chunky nose at me and frowned. "Didn't your mama teach you any manners?" she questioned, planting both her hands on her chubby hips.

Why is she trying me?! I took a deep breath and said seriously, "Don't worry about what my mama taught me. Now mind your business." I continued.

"It's hot-in-the-ass girls like you that have the STD rate booming in the community!"

No she didn't! I wanted to inform her that I use protection and I get tested regularly, but it was a wasted discussion. Instead, I took the low road and followed up with an insult. "And it's fat asses like you that have the obesity rate soaring in our country!" I snapped. The look in her eyes told me I had struck a nerve.

"Just be careful," she said in a low growl.

"Thank you. I will," I said pleasantly. *Nothin' like killin' 'em with kindness.*

"I was talking to *him,*" she said sarcastically, pointing to Deon. At that, she shook her head and waddled off, pushing the grocery cart in front of her.

Exhaling loudly, I turned back to Deon. He was

laughing and shaking his head. "You're bad." He chuckled.

"You have no idea," I said sweetly. "Now, where were we?" I asked.

"We were discussing dinner… and melons."

"Oh, that's right." I smiled, snapping my fingers. "Your place or mine?"

"Yours," he answered a bit too quickly.

Maybe it was my intuition secretly whispering at me or that redhead had a point about strangers, but I hesitated for a brief moment before I said, "Sure." What can I say? I've never been very good at listening to my intuition. Besides, what did Big Red know? After all, she was a stranger! I gave him my address and my number, paid for my groceries, and glided out of the supermarket, carrying my bags and wearing a smile.

* * * * *

I've never been very good at cooking. In fact, I suck big time when it comes to the kitchen. So, for my meal with Deon, I made a stop by Chin Chin restaurant and purchased appetizers and a main course. I dimmed the lights in my dining room and lit my vanilla scented candles and sat them on the floor around the room. The light from the candles reflected off the eggplant color on the walls, giving the illusion of rippling waves of water.

After setting the table, I bounced upstairs to bathe and get dressed.

My doorbell rang at exactly eight o'clock. I ran downstairs wearing a simple but sexy red strapless above-the-knee Juicy Couture dress and gold four-inch stilettos. I opened the door and smiled.

Deon wore crisp jeans and a pink button-down shirt. I was impressed because not many men can wear pink, but Deon wore it well. He held a bottle of wine in one hand and a bouquet of red roses in the other. "Damn." He smiled, scanning me with his eyes.

"You like?"

"Most definitely!" He handed me the roses and stepped through the doorway into the living room.

"Thank you." I shut the door before giving him a big hug.

His hands slid down the curve of my back to the top of my ass. I could sense he wanted to go lower, but he didn't. Instead, he held me tightly for a moment and then let me go. "Nice place," he said, looking around my living room. His eyes landed directly on the pole. He looked from the pole to me and then back at the pole. "Do I get dinner and a show?" he asked with his eyebrows raised.

"Play your cards right, and you just may." I smiled, batting my eyes.

"Something smells good."

"Besides me?" I flirted, leading him to the dining room.

"Yes," He laughed.

I looked over my shoulder at him and saw his eyes were locked on my ass. I put an extra twist in my model walk to give him a tad more eye candy. "Have a seat." I smiled, pointing to one of the dining room chairs. "I'll be right back." I excused myself to the kitchen, retrieved a crystal vase from under the sink, and partially filled it with water. After placing my roses in the vase, I sat them on the windowsill above my sink.

I returned to the dining room carrying a platter of hacked spicy chicken, shrimp cocktail, flavored cucumbers, and spicy cabbage. Deon had the wine open and both our glasses filled. "I hope you like Chinese." I smiled, placing the tray in the middle of the table.

"I love Chinese."

"Wonderful." I sat down opposite him at the table.

"So, who is Marylin?" he asked.

"Oh, I'm a simple girl." I smiled. "Born and raised in the South." I cut the discussion off with those few words, but Deon's eyes told me he wanted to know more. My eyes told him that was all he was getting.

"You don't like to share, huh?" he said coolly.

"I guess you can say I'm a private person." I gave him

a small smile. I wanted him to know I wasn't upset, but I was not about to tell him my life story. If I did, I would have to kill him, and I was saving that sin for someone else. The two of us were not going to have a long-term relationship; in fact, I planned on this being our last meal together. There really was no need for either of us to delve any deeper, whether he realized it or not.

"Well, I'm an open book," he said. "Ask me anything."

"Why don't we just enjoy our dinner?" I suggested. "I'm sure your story is a wonderful one, but I'd rather just enjoy our night," I said sweetly.

"We can do that," he said with a smile.

I exhaled, grateful he wasn't ultra-sensitive. I would hate for our night to end before it got started.

From then on, our conversation was a general one. We talked about the weather, traffic, and politics. We finished our appetizers and our main course, which consisted of duck drizzled in orange sauce and eggplant. After that, I invited Deon to have a seat in the living room while I slipped upstairs to freshen up.

* * * * *

I slipped my favorite mixed CD into my CD player, turned up the volume, and stepped slowly down the staircase. I wore see-through platform heels, a red lace thong, and a matching red lace bra.

Deon watched me with a smile plastered on his face. His expression reminded me of a child who had just been awarded an extra scoop of his favorite ice cream with a cherry on top.

The sound of Maxwell singing "Bad Habits" flowed like liquid seduction through my surround-sound system. I winked my eye at Deon and then stepped up onto the platform surrounding the pole. I held onto the pole with one hand, while taking small steps around it in a circle. I stopped with my ass resting against the cold metal and then slid my legs out in front of me. Arching my back, I rotated and rolled my hips slowly. My motions were fluent, like a fish moving gracefully underwater. I spread my legs shoulder width apart, continuing to grind my hips in the air. I moved to my own rhythm, and for a moment, there was only me and Maxwell in the room. I pulled myself up to stand upright and then pulled myself up onto the pole. Wrapping my ankles around the top of the pole, I let go, allowing myself to hang upside down.

"Damn."

The sound of Deon's voice reminded me I had an audience. Opening my eyes, I focused on him. Pulling myself up into a full split, I slid down to the floor. Rolling up onto my knees, I crawled slowly over to the sofa. Placing my hands on Deon's knees, I climbed up into his lap. His eyes sparkled like diamonds. Smiling, I straddled his waist and began to grind against his crotch seductively. Deon grabbed my hips and relaxed against the sofa. I could feel him growing inside of his pants, and I loved the feel of his hard on. Unbuttoning his shirt slowly, I continued to massage my crotch against his. I pushed the material open, unveiling Deon's chiseled chest and abs. Running my fingertips along his skin, I traced the pattern of his pecks with my nails. Leaning in, I traced my tongue around the rim of his earlobe, blowing lightly. I felt his nature pulsating below me. "Are you ready?" I asked, flicking my tongue across his lips.

"Can't you tell?" His voice was low and winded.

"How do you want it, Daddy?"

"I can show you better than I can tell you." He stood with me wrapped tightly around his waist and then moved quickly up the staircase.

Chapter 6

(Essence)

After Andrew left for training, I hurried downstairs to my private office that Andrew had created to give me a space to work on my designs and conduct my business. The room was filled with fabric samples, a drawing table, a sewing table, and a large desk with built-in file cabinets. Inside the file cabinets, I kept design layouts and private information from my past.

I plopped down in the leather high-back chair and slid behind the mahogany desk. I felt along the bottom of the desk until I found the key I kept taped underneath. Once I had the cabinet unlocked, I removed the small metal lockbox I had hidden under several folders and bundles of paperwork. I quickly entered the combination and flipped the top open. Removing the small leather-bound book, I exhaled while thinking of my mysterious caller. *What else does he know?* He hadn't mentioned any other information about the past. It didn't make any sense. Cracking the book open, I took a journey into my past.

* * * * *

I was thrown into the foster care system at the age of twelve, after my mother was murdered by one of her boyfriends. My mother, Savannah, was one of the most beautiful and baddest women in our neighborhood. She was five-six and 125 pounds with curves so dangerous they should have come with a warning label. She had smooth, caramel-colored skin and hair that hung in a bounty of curls past her shoulders. She had the looks of a model and the brains of a teacher. Her downfall, however, was her love of money and the men she used to get it. I remember my mother had two main men she kept on her team: her 'Sunday go-to-meetin brother' and her 'He's just a friend'.

The 'Sunday go-to-meetin' brother' was a tall, Wesley Snipes-looking man by the name of Franklin. Franklin came through every Sunday after conducting morning worship service at the I Have Faith Worship Center, where Mama and I attended church occasionally. As the pastor of I Have Faith, Franklin stood in the pulpit and preached of hell and damnation until people in the congregation were screaming and shouting. Then, every Sunday evening after service, he came over to our apartment, ate the home-cooked meal Mama prepared for us, and then the two of them slipped into Mama's bedroom, where it was his turn to do the screaming and shouting. Afterwards, Franklin always gave Mama a love offering, better known as the rent. "God bless," he always said, and then he went on his way. Franklin was fond of Mama, but he had to keep a certain image for his congregation, and she wasn't exactly pastor's wife material. She believed in showing off her curves, and she was sharp tongued and quick tempered. Franklin once made the mistake of asking her to tone it down, and Mama looked him in his eyes with her hands planted firmly on her hips and said, "If God didn't want me to put all this on display, He wouldn't have created the masterpiece, and when He decides I no longer need to have this attitude, He will stop sending people my way that piss me off!"

'He's just a friend' was the name given to every other random man Mama used to fund her hair, nails, and wardrobe. Whenever she was asked about who the men were to her, she simply replied, "He's just a friend." My birth father was also placed somewhere in this category. Mama explained that he knew where I was if he wanted me, and if he didn't want to get to know me it was his lost and not mine. Unlike the children you read about who grow up with issues of repression and abandonment, I was cool without knowing the man. It's my personal belief that you can't miss something you never had.

My mother had all of her men exactly where she wanted them—wrapped right around her perfect little fingers. But sadly for her, this all changed one blistery Wednesday night in December.

I sat on our living room floor, drawing in my new sketch pad that William (the current 'He's just a friend') had bought for me. The loud bangs on our front door pulled my attention away from what I was doing. I assumed it was either our next-door neighbor Vita or her daughter Cecily coming to borrow something again, but I assumed wrong.

"Where's your mama?" Franklin asked, storming through our front door and stepping past me. He was dressed that night in a long black trench coat and his traditional pinstripe suit and hat. His expression was unreadable, but I knew his presence was not a good sign. First, Franklin never came by without calling, and second, Mama and William had been locked up in her room for the majority of the night.

"She went out with Vita," I lied quickly.

"Humph," he grumbled.

"Don't ya'll have Bible study on Wednesdays?" I asked, attempting to change the subject.

"Every Wednesday," he said lowly.

I watched Franklin as he scanned the living room with his eyes. *You gotta get him outta here,* I thought to myself. "We have to come one Wednesday," I said, nodding my head. "Mama should be back in a couple of hours. "I'll tell her you stopped through." I smiled nervously and held the door open, hoping he'd take the hint.

He looked at me and then at the hallway that led to Mama's bedroom, a route he knew well.

Leave. Please leave.

Franklin moved slowly but finally started walking back toward the door. I held my breath, ready to exhale when he left, but the sound of Mama's moaning disrupted our silence. Franklin looked like someone had punched him in the chest and pulled out his heart. I prayed the best way I knew how as he marched through our living room down the hall to Mama's bedroom, with me following close on his heels. Franklin opened the door to reveal Mama's and William's bodies entwined in what would be their last moment of intimacy.

"Franklin!" Mama yelled, pulling the sheet up around her breasts. "Baby?" she asked, looking at me.

"Mama—"

I was cut off by William. "What the fuck?" he yelled, struggling to get out of the bed.

Pop!

He never made it.

My ears rang terribly as I watched William slump back down on the bed from the bullet that ripped through his chest.

Mama stared at William's lifeless body. Her face looked almost angelic, although it was covered with splatters of William's blood. "What are you doing?!" she screamed.

"A gracious woman retaineth honor," Franklin mumbled, pointing the gun at Mama.

I wanted to scream, to beg Franklin not to kill my mama, but the words were muffled, swallowed by my fear of what was coming next.

"Our Father, which art in Heaven," Franklin rambled.

Pop! Pop!

"Noooo!!!" I screamed as tears streamed down my cheeks. I sobbed uncontrollably as I stood frozen in place.

"Lord have mercy," I heard Franklin say.

Pop!

I shivered as pieces of Franklin's brains and warm blood fell upon me like tainted rain.

After my mother's death, I was placed in Angel's House, a group home for children. There, I was schooled and taught by a group of Catholic nuns. Many families were interested in adopting me, but none of them were ever deemed suitable enough to be my family, or at least that's what I was told. One night after hearing a couple of the sisters talking, I learned the truth: They didn't want a child who had experienced what I had lived through. I came with too much baggage, and they didn't feel I was worth the risk.

I eventually grew content with staying in Angel's House. I had a roof over my head, and I became somewhat of a teacher's pet to Sister Mary Thomas, the head mistress. Sister Mary Thomas took me under her wing during my stay at Angel's House, and she encouraged me to study hard and was my personal tutor when it came down to the subjects of foreign language and art. Just as I had with my birth mother, I absorbed every lesson she taught like a sponge. For four years, Sister Mary Thomas was a new mother to me until cancer took her life. I was devastated and heartbroken when she passed, but then the Abernathys came along.

The first year with Ian and Emma Abernathy was wonderful. Emma, a pretty, heavyset woman with dark skin and short, curly hair, worked as a nurse. Ian was a tall, handsome, slender man with olive-colored skin and light green eyes, an electrician. Our first year together was wonderful. I was their only child, and because Emma couldn't bare children of her own, I was the center of their attention. I went to school and always came home to find dinner and a smile waiting for me. I never knew my own father, but I finally had a father figure in Ian, or so I thought. Things slowly began to change after my seventeenth birthday.

I was a late bloomer physically, but by the age of seventeen, I was practically a living replica of my mother. I had the same beautiful facial features and curvaceous body. I captured the attention of men young and old, including Ian. His behavior toward me slowly began to change. He went from treating me like his daughter to acting like an overprotective lover. Whenever he took me shopping for new clothes, he would insist on hanging outside the dressing rooms while I changed. A couple of times, I caught him peeking over the dressing room doors at me. But the shopping sprees were only the beginning.

One night, I woke up and found Ian hovering over my bed, reeking of alcohol and massaging himself through his boxers. "What are you doing?" I asked, pulling the covers up around my neck.

"Thought I heard something," he mumbled. He stood there for a few seconds, looking at me with this eerie look in his eyes, then, without another word, he turned and walked out of the room. At first I was freaked out by his behavior but I later charged his odd behavior off as drunken sleepwalking.

It wasn't until after I had returned from a date that everything changed for the worst. I had just walked through the front door of our home after kissing Darius, my first boyfriend, goodnight. Darius was a pretty boy of Black and Puerto Rican descent. He had warm brown eyes, wavy hair the color of tar, and was tall with nice biceps. The living room was dark, but I knew as soon as I shut the front door behind me that I was not alone.

"How was it?" Ian's words were slurred.

I flipped the light switch on so I could look at him. He sat on the plush sofa, dressed only in a wife beater and boxers. A half-empty pint of Seagram's gin sat on the coffee table in front of him.

"I had fun." I gave him a faint smile.

His eyes traveled from mine down the curve of my body to my white Nikes. I was glad I had adjusted my fitted sweater and jeans before I climbed out of Darius's Honda Accord. The way Ian was scanning me with his eyes, I was sure he would have snapped if even a thread was out of place. "Did he have fun?" he asked. He rubbed the brittle patch of hair along his chin, never taking his eyes off me.

"Yeah. The movie was really funny." I suddenly felt like I was standing under a microscope; Ian's eyes darted from my face to my breasts and then down to my crotch.

"Did he touch you?" he asked.

"What do you mean?"

"You know…*touch* you.," he whispered through clenched teeth.

"Just my hand," I lied.

"Did he kiss you?" he asked, snatching the bottle off the table. He took a long sip and then set the bottle back down.

"I should go to bed," I said, quickly changing the subject.

"Boys like that come and go," he said, letting out a low belch. "They get what they want, and then they move on to the next one."

"Darius hasn't pressured me to do anything."

"Maybe not yet," he snapped, "but soon he will." He rubbed his disheveled hair carelessly. I watched as he stroked his locks over and over in rapid succession. "And you'll give it to him," he said, staring at me. His eyes filled with water, signaling the onset of tears.

"Ian, I don't want to have sex with Darius or anyone else for that matter," I said reassuringly, "so you can stop worrying yourself about it." This was true, as I had every intention of holding onto my virginity with a vice grip. I knew what I had in between my legs was a treasure, and

I was in no hurry to share my wealth.

He wiped his eyes with the back of his hand. "Choose me," he said softly.

"What?"

"Me." His eyes lowered to small slits. "I'll divorce Emma. We can have babies." He stood and moved in close to me—too close. He was so close his lips were mere inches from my face.

I took a quick step back. "Ian, you're drunk," I said.

"I know what I'm saying," he said. "I'm in love with you. Please choose me."

"This isn't right," I said, trying to reason with him. I stepped to move around him, but he grabbed my elbow to stop me.

"I need you," he whined, pulling me against his body. The scent of alcohol mixed with sweat seeped from his pores, causing me to gag slightly.

"I just want to go to bed," I said.

"Let me go with you."

"She's going alone," Emma spoke firmly.

I snatched away from Ian's grip and moved quickly to her side.

She wore a long powder blue housecoat with matching slippers. Her hair was wrapped in a multi-color scarf. "Go to your room," she said softly.

I nodded my head and walked past her, up the long

hallway to my bedroom. Once I was within the security of my bedroom, I sat down on the bed. I listened, expecting to hear an explosive exchange of words, but instead their voices were low whispers. After fifteen minutes, I heard the door to their bedroom shut and a soft tap on my door.

"It's me," Emma said softly.

I quickly unlocked the door to let her in. "Are you okay?" I asked.

"I'm fine," she said, shutting the door behind her, "but we need to talk about what happened tonight. Sit down," she said sweetly.

I sat back down on the bed and looked up at her.

"Ian told me what happened," she said softly.

I was relieved. I sat anxiously, waiting for her to tell me that he was a sick bastard, and first thing in the morning, the doorknob would be hitting him in the crack of his ass.

"I know everything that's been going on, but I forgive you."

"Wh-what?" I thought I heard her incorrectly. "Forgive *me?* For what?" I asked.

"Ian told me you've been acting inappropriately with him," she explained, "that you're confused about your feelings for him."

I couldn't believe what I was hearing and that Emma

actually believed it. "That's not true!" I said, shaking my head. "He's been doing things—"

"Tatiana, I understand you may be confused about your feelings," she said, cutting me off. "Ian is the first man to show you genuine love and affection. However, his feelings for you are strictly those a man has for his daughter."

"Emma, he said he is in love with me—that he would divorce you!" I rambled. "He said he wants me to have his babies!"

"I will not listen to your lies!" She snapped. "Ian is a good man!"

"But you heard him saying he wanted to go to bed with me!" I attempted to reason with her.

"He didn't mean it that way," she said, crossing her arms across her breasts. " You have to stop this. I will not let you destroy my marriage!"

"What?" I snapped back. "Your fucking husband came on to me!" I had never disrespected Emma before, but at that moment, my heart was hurting, and when my heart aches, my tongue has a habit of lashing out with venom that would make a spitting cobra jealous.

"You are a whore," she said, "just like your mother."

The mere mention of my mother caused anger to burn inside me, hotter than a thousand fiery furnaces. "And you're stupid," I said, standing. "That's why you can't have your own damn kids," I said sarcastically. "No child deserves a fucked-up father who wants to screw them and a dumb-ass mother!"

Before I could blink or flinch, Emma slapped me so hard I saw stars swirling before my eyes. I instinctively balled up my fist, prepared to go to war. We stared at each other in silence until she finally said, "I want you out of my house…. tonight." She looked at me one last time and then left the room.

* * * * *

Two hours later, I stood behind the large oak tree outside my bedroom with my Nike backpack on my shoulder and my small overnight bag in my hand. Stuffed inside the front pocket of my jeans was $300 I had managed to save up from my allowance, plus $257 I snatched from the cookie jar Emma kept hidden in the pantry. I strolled down the street, leaving the memories shared with Emma and Ian behind, and from then on, I was officially on my own.

I didn't have any way to call Darius, but I knew he would be home alone. His father worked third shift for the City of Huntsville Police Department, and his mother was out of town visiting her family in Puerto Rico. I figured I would stay the night with him, and then the two of us could figure out what my next move would be in the morning. These hopes were quickly dashed when I peeked through Darius's bedroom window to see him butt-ass naked, screwing the hell out of Chelsea Massey, the captain of the cheerleading squad and one of my closest friends. My first instinct was to kick both their asses, but the truth is, deep inside, I always knew Darius was too fine to be keeping his dick to himself. I also knew Chelsea was a bona fide high school ho. She had been passed around our high school basketball team more times than a Spaulding on the court. I pulled myself from the X-rated show Darius and Chelsea were giving. I decided to handle the situation like a good girl, but not before I let all the air out of Darius's tires and scratched the word 'Bitch' on the hood of his Accord. Hey, sometimes good girls do bad things.

I was lost in my own thoughts when the black four-door Caddy with dark tinted windows pulled up alongside me. I gripped my overnight bag close to my body and nonchalantly slipped my hand through the opening, grasping the end of the butcher knife I had nabbed in the Abernathy's kitchen.

The driver's side window slowly came down. "Need some help?"

"I'm good," I said, continuing my stroll.

"You need a ride or something?" he asked. His voice was smooth as silk.

I turned, and our eyes locked.

He smiled a smile so sweet it could have melted chocolate on a cold winter's night. "Are you in some kind of trouble?" His brown eyes sparkled as he continued to drive alongside me.

"No." I shuffled my overnight bag from one hand to the other. "Why would you think that?" I knew if he was a cop or an overly concerned citizen, I would end up downtown at the fifth precinct.

"Well, it's one in the morning," he said, "and you're carrying bags."

"I'm just passing through," I said.

"Where are you headed?" he prodded.

"I'm going to catch a bus ." I was weaving my web of lies as the seconds ticked by.

"To where?" he questioned.

"Why are you asking?" I asked impatiently. "Are you with the police or something?"

Shaking his head, he laughed lightly. "No, no. I'm just concerned," he said. "It's rough out here in the streets."

"I can handle my own," I informed him.

He stopped the car and then got out. I moved further down the street to put some distance between us, but then I stopped. He looked like he was in his early twenties. He wore dark jeans, creased to perfection, and a green polo shirt. His brown skin was flawless. "Let me give you a ride to the station," he said, taking a step forward.

"I'm good," I said.

"Look, I'm not going to leave you out here alone," he insisted, "so, if you won't ride with me, I'll just have to walk with you." I watched as he walked back to the car, killed the engine, and locked the door. At the time, I didn't know if he was crazy or a genuinely good guy. "Let's go," he said, smiling at me.

"You know, there have been a lot of good Samaritans in history who have turned up dead!" I teased.

"Well, when it's your time to go, you go."

"That's real," I said, "but you don't have to rush it along."

"Look, we can either ride in the comfort of my whip, or we can get our stroll on," he said, staring at me. "It's your choice."

"Okay, I'll ride with you!" I exhaled. I don't know how I knew, but something told me I was safe with him.

As the two of us approached the Greyhound station, he told me his name was JT and that he was from Detroit and had come to Huntsville to visit his family.

I explained why I was running away and confessed that I had no real destination.

"I figured that."

"How?" I asked curiously.

"Because the last bus out of Da'Ville left an hour

ago." He laughed.

"Damn! Why didn't you just say that?"

"Because I told you I would take you where you wanted to go," he said, looking over at me, "and I'm nothing if not a man of my word."

"Hmm. I can respect that," I said.

"So, what are your plans?" he asked. "You got people you can stay with?"

"Nope," I confessed. "Just me, myself, and I."

"You ever been to the D?"

"Never."

"You wanna roll wit' me?"

"And do what?" I questioned. My faith in mankind was justifiably a bit rattled at the moment.

"My boy will give you a job," he said, "in his club."

"What kind of club?" I asked curiously.

"Strip joint," he said, "but I'll get him to put you behind the bar and set you up with a place to live."

"It'll be a new beginning," he said.

"I sure could use a new beginning," I said, considering his offer.

"So, what's up?"

I thought about it for a second and finally concluded things couldn't get any worse. "Let's go," I said.

Chapter 7

(Essence)

JT stayed true to his word. He introduced me to Carlos, who was the owner of Club Delow. Carlos was a handsome man with skin the color of dark chocolate, light brown eyes, and a smooth bald head. When it came down to policies and procedures, Carlos only had one; get money.

My career at Delow began with me working the bar four nights a week. When I wasn't working the bar, I sat in the club observing the dancers working the pole. Occasionally, I sat by the stage assisting the girls and observing how they interacted with the patrons of the club. I quickly learned at Club Delow that men were suckers for a pretty face, a phat ass, and nice titties. However, looks combined with a slick mouthpiece made a woman damn near irresistible. This is how one of the top girls at the club managed to take home over a grand every week.

Destiny, as she called herself, was the Club Delow feature dancer, a cute chocolate sista. At five-seven, Destiny had legs for days and a banging body. Whenever she stepped onto the stage, the crowd went wild and made it rain. The money I was getting for working the bar was good, but I knew it could be better. So, when Destiny accidentally slipped stepping on stage and unfortunately broke her leg, I saw it as the perfect opportunity for me to step my game up.

"Fuck!" I heard Carlos scream from inside his office. "Six weeks? I can't believe my bottom bitch is out for six weeks!" I stood outside his office eavesdropping. I listened to Carlos rant, rave, and scream about how much money would be lost without his feature.

"We can always put someone else in." I recognized the second voice, which belonged to Dre', one of Carlos's wingmen. Dre' was responsible for looking after all the dancers. He made sure they showed up on time and that they had their shit together. At five-seven and 170 pounds, Dre' favored Will Smith in the face. His attitude, however, was as shitty as they come. The way he walked around and gave orders with his chest poked out, you would have sworn he owned the place. The truth was, all Carlos had to do was speak, and Dre' was the first one to back down like a little bitch.

"Like who?" Carlos asked.

"What about Ecstasy?" Dre' suggested.

I silently laughed at the thought. The girl was paper thin and danced like she had cement blocks attached to her ankles.

"You shitting me, right?" Carlos barked. "That ho ain't making no real money. Hell, the only reason she still here is because she's your family." He continued, "If I'm going to have a feature, she's got to be a class act."

I saw this as my chance and knocked lightly on the door.

"Whoever it is, now is not your time!" Carlos yelled.

I could hear the anger in his voice, but I decided to take my chances.

"Yo, I know you didn't just open my mutha f—" Carlos stopped when he saw me step through the door. "Now's not the time," Carlos said. He was sitting behind his desk, rubbing his fingertips back and forth across his temples.

Dre' sat across from the desk. He looked at me like I had lost my mind for entering the office without permission.

I decided not to waste any time explaining myself. "I know someone who can be the new feature," I said quickly.

Carlos continued to massage his temples as he stared

at me.

I shifted my weight from one leg to the other. I won't lie: I was nervous as hell, but I had gone too far to turn back.

"Oh yeah?" Carlos said. "And who'd you have in mind?"

I gave him a small smile. "Me," I said.

Dre' burst out laughing, but I ignored him.

Carlos relaxed in his chair and looked at me. "You want to hit the stage, huh?"

Dre' laughed. "You can't be serious."

"I'm very serious," I said, rolling my eyes at him.

"We ain't got time for this shit," Dre' said. "We'll holler. Shut the door behind you."

"Slow yo roll," Carlos said, looking at Dre'.

Dre' sat back in his chair like a whipped puppy. I wanted to commend him on his obedience by patting his head and saying *'Good boy'*, but I decided against it.

"You ever danced before?" Carlos asked.

I could tell he was considering the possibility, but I had to try to keep my composure. "No, but I've been watching the other girls," I began.

"So that makes you an expert?" Dre' questioned.

"No, but I'm a quick learner," I said, speaking directly to Carlos. "Look how fast I learned the bar."

"True," Carlos agreed, "but taking your clothes off for

a bunch of horny mutha fuckers is a whole new game."

"I can handle it," I said confidently.

Carlos nodded his head. "I'll give you a week to practice," he said. "Next Friday, you'll audition for me. If I like what I see, you're my new feature. Deal?" he asked, eyeing me.

I smiled victoriously. "Deal," I said. I turned to leave the office when Dre' called my name. "What's up?" I asked, looking at him.

"You were right there when Destiny tripped," he said. "How'd it happen?" he asked.

I knew what he was insinuating, and he was correct. "She was going up the steps, and she tripped over her feet," I lied.

"Yeah, but with you being so close, seems to me you would have been able to help cushion her fall," he said, eyeing me.

"I reached out to her," I said lowly.

"Why didn't I see you?" he asked.

"I don't know," I said. "Maybe because you were busy up in Asia's face."

Carlos's eyebrows shot up, and Dre' looked completely busted. I had been watching Dre' flirt with one of the girls all night, so I knew when was the right time to make my move. However, somehow he still knew I played a part in Destiny's fall. The truth was, I tripped her. Destiny was so high she didn't know what happened. She said one minute she was stepping up on the stage, and the next she felt her leg go back the wrong way and she was hitting the stage face first. You'd think with all the practice she had in heels, she would at least know how to break her fall, but the ho came tumbling down like Humpty Dumpty off the brick wall. Yeah, it was a low blow, but that's life. Only the realest bitches survive.

"Look, bi—" Dre' started, standing up.

"Sit yo ass down!" Carlos ordered.

Just like a faithful pound puppy, Dre' did as he was told.

"Tatiana, I'll get Zoe to hook you up with something to practice in."

I smiled brightly. "Thank you," I said.

"You can go for now," he said, cutting his eyes at Dre'. "We got some shit to discuss."

I gave Dre' a small smirk before walking out the door.

* * * * *

That week leading up to my audition with Carlos, I practiced my ass off, and by the time Friday came, my confidence was off the charts. Carlos always conducted interviews with Dre', JT, and another one of his partners,

Damien, before the club opened. All the men took their seats by the stage.

Zoe, who happened to be one of Carlos's many boosters around town, hooked me up with a purple lace corset, along with a matching thong and stilletos. I looked and felt unstoppable. I stepped out on the stage, and immediately the men's mouths dropped open—all except for one of them.

"Damn," Damien said, smiling. "Shawty thick-ass shit."

"Hell yeah," JT chimed in, staring at me.

I gave him a sweet smile. Since he had brought me to Detroit and got me the job at Club Delow, JT and I had become very close. At that time, he treated me like a sister, but eventually the two of us became lovers.

Dre' looked uninterested, but I could tell by the way his eyes grazed from my face to my toes that he, too, liked what he saw.

Carlos looked at me, with a straight face. "Audition closed," he said, watching me.

"What?" JT asked, looking at Carlos.

"Don't make me say it again," Carlos barked.

There were a few moans and groans as JT and Damien slowly rose from their chairs.

"Dre', start the music before you go," Carlos ordered.

Dre' looked from Carlos to me. "But I always sit in,"

he said, looking at Carlos.

"Not today," Carlos said.

I giggled to myself and waited for Dre' to start the music before grudgingly making his exit. Jodeci's "Feenin'" blasted through the stereo speakers as I began to work the pole. I had watched the other girls enough that I was able to steal some of their moves and make them my own. One of my favorites was Destiny's signature move, where she flipped off the pole backwards. I took that, too, only I perfected it. When I flipped off the pole, I landed in the splits and then pulled myself up into a handstand. After popping up out of my handstand, I stepped slowly over to the side of the stage where Carlos sat, watching my every move. I slowly eased myself down on his lap and began to grind slowly. Our eyes locked as I rotated my hips seductively. I wrapped my hands around his neck and slowly bent backwards, pushing my breasts in his face. I eased back up and wrapped my legs around his shoulders. I swirled my hips, grinding against his chest. When I felt the growth in his pants, I raised myself up until I was straddling him and looking him directly in his eyes. I reached down to the hooks on my corset, prepared to go topless and show him what I was working with.

Carlos grabbed my hands, preventing me from going any further, and the music stopped. "Club Delow has a new feature," he said. "You start tomorrow."

I smiled victoriously.

"You got a stage name?" he asked, easing me off his lap.

I shook my head.

"From here on out, you'll be known as Jade," he said.

"I like that," I said with a proud smile. "Jade. Yeah, I like that a lot."

Chapter 8

(Essence)

One year later, I was the club favorite. Being the Club Delow number one girl brought me an array of admirers, along with enough money to purchase my first car and rent myself a nice three-bedroom townhome on the west side of Detroit. It felt good to maintain my own, but at times it felt like there was something or someone reaching out to me. It wasn't until I received the phone call that I understood what that something was.

"Hello," I answered while dabbing my face with a towel. I had just finished working the pole to R. Kelly's "Sex Me" when Shay, the bar manager, advised me I had a call. I slipped into the dressing room for privacy. I assumed it was yet another Delow patron wanting me to go out with them. I hadn't—and never would—take any of them up on their offers, but I still accepted the calls. Although, I didn't believe in fraternizing with the club patrons outside of work, there was no rhyme nor reason to being rude. Besides, having a jacked-up attitude would fuck with my money, and I don't play when it comes down to my money.

"Hey," the female voice said from the other end of the phone.

"Who is this?"

"It's me, Tay Tay," she said, clearing her throat.

I hadn't been called Tay Tay since I was a child. The old nickname brought back memories of my days at Monrovia, the elementary school I attended in Huntsville. "Who is this?" I asked again.

"It's me, Tanya."

"Tanya?"

"Yes! How are you?" she asked cheerfully.

"I'm good," I said slowly. "How are you?"

"I'm great." She laughed with the same squeaky laugh she had when we were children—the kind that made *me* want to laugh, even if the situation wasn't funny. Although the two of us had grown up and gone our separate ways, her laugh still brought a smile to my face.

"How did you know where to find me?" I asked.

Tanya and I hadn't seen each other since I was sent

to Angel's House after my mother's murder. In fact, we hadn't had time to say goodbye. There was just too much tragedy surrounding that night. When the social worker came to the apartment, I grabbed my things and never looked back. I had forgotten the friends and loved ones I had left behind. I guess in some way, it was my own personal way of dealing with what had taken place.

"I saw pictures of you on the Internet," she said.

"Damn! I didn't know I was out there like that," I said, shaking my head. I made a mental note to do a search on myself later.

"Yep," she laughed, "But you look good, Tay."

"Thanks."

"I would like to see you," she said. "I miss you, Tay-Tay."

It's amazing how we can go years without seeing someone and then, for whatever reason, they decide they want to pop back up and mend broken ties. It may be a lover, a parent, or a childhood best friend, and although we've built new lives without them, we still feel a certain connection to them. I guess there are some people from our past that, no matter how far we've grown apart, we will always welcome them with open arms. Tanya was one of those people for me. "I miss you too," I said. "Tell me the address there."

Chapter 9

(Essence)

I thought moving Tanya to Detroit to live with me was a good idea, and for the first six months, it was. We did everything together. We were more than best friends; we were family. Carlos gave her a job working at Club Delow, and together we became the Dynamic Duo. I didn't mind sharing the spotlight with Tanya. It was always about the money with me, not about the fame. She adjusted to working the pole, but she was always better at working the floor and interacting with the customers. She had her flirt game down pat, and I respected her for it. I've never been the type to knock another woman's hustle.

Since Tanya was holding her own and bringing in enough money to go in on half of our living expenses, I decided to go to school. I cut back on my hours at the club and enrolled in the International Academy of Design and Technology, selecting fashion design as my major. It was then that things started to unravel.

One night while I was in class, Tanya sent me a text letting me know she was going to catch a ride home with one of the girls from the club. I decided this was the perfect opportunity for me to get some much needed TLC. After all, JT and I hadn't had any real time together since Tanya moved in, and I desperately needed to get laid.

The two of us had just finished round two of our sexual reunion when JT brought up Tanya. "Your girl has gotten real tight with Ecstasy and Dre'," he said, stroking my hair.

I lay with my face pressed against his chest. "Really?" I asked, propping myself up on my elbow. Tanya hadn't mentioned developing a friendship with Ecstasy nor Dre'. I didn't have a problem with Ecstasy, per se, but I knew she made a lot of her decisions based on Dre's influence, and Dre' was a straight-up asshole. He would use his own mama to put a dollar in his pocket.

"Yep. Shawty been spending a lot of time in the back room on the nights you ain't there."

"Why you just now telling me?" I asked, sitting up and looking over at him. The only girls in the club that went into the back room were the ones turning tricks. In my whole entire career at Delow, I had not even so much as sneezed in the direction of the back room. I wanted my money, but I wasn't about to give no man or woman head for a damn dollar.

"You know I don't like that snitch shit," he said, sitting up. "I hollered at Tanya about it, and she told me she was just in there giving lap dances. Hell, I didn't have any proof proving otherwise, so I let it ride." I watched as he reached over onto the floor and pulled a rolled blunt out of his shirt pocket. He lit it up and took a long pull. "Then tonight, when I heard she was going to go party with them," he said, exhaling slowly, "I thought maybe I should speak up." He hit the blunt again and then offered it to me.

"I'm good." I had never smoked in my life, but I didn't care if my friends did. I had nothing against a good contact buzz. "Party where?" My mind instantly started to wonder.

"At Dre's," he said, coughing slightly.

"She's at *Dre's* house?" I asked, climbing off the bed. I walked over to my armoire and pulled out a clean tank top and a pair of shorts. I knew Dre' was bad news, and I had heard he liked to dabble in all kinds of activities, from treating his nose with cocaine to setting women out and making low-budget porn. At one point, the Detroit PD had even run up in Delow and dragged his sorry ass downtown for questioning. When I asked one of the girls what it was in regards to, she said they had been tipped off that he was having sex and setting out twelve-year-old girls. It's one thing when it's a grownup who is willing to participate, but it takes a despicable human being to run up in a child. They dropped the charges because they didn't have enough evidence, but deep in my heart, I always felt Dre' was guilty.

"Baby, what you doing?" JT asked, looking at me.

"I'm 'bout to go over to his crib and get my family," I said, looking at him.

"You can't do that," he said, putting the blunt out.

"Why can't I ?" I snapped.

"One, because Tanya is a grown-ass woman," he said, "and two, because you going over there ain't stopping her from doing what she want to do…and three, because I'm still horny."

I rolled my eyes at him while trying hard not to laugh.

"Come here," he said, extending his arms out to me.

I stood still for a moment considering the reasons he had provided. He was right. I wasn't Tanya's mother, and I couldn't forbid her from going anywhere. I opted to just speak with her about the situation and go from there. Dropping my clothes on the floor, I climbed back into the bed and settled into JT's arms.

"Don't worry, boo. I'm sure she'll be home soon," he said, kissing my neck.

* * * * *

Twenty- four hours later, I was blowing Tanya's cell phone up. I hadn't heard nor seen her, and I was sick to my stomach with worry. I had even attempted to call Ecstasy and Dre'. Ecstasy's phone was turned off, and Dre' kept sending me to voicemail. I had just stopped pacing across the living room floor when Tanya came through the door, carrying her gym bag. "Where you been?" I snapped, staring at her.

She looked at me and smiled. Reaching into the bag, she pulled out a roll of twenties secured with a rubber band. "Getting that money," she said.

"I've been blowing your phone up," I said. "I was worried sick, Tanya."

"I *know* you been blowing me up," she said, rolling her eyes. "You ran down my battery." She stared at me like she was waiting for an apology.

"Well, if you had returned my calls or at least sent a courtesy text, I would have stopped calling."

"I appreciate the concern," she said, "but you take care of you. I got me."

No she didn't! I thought to myself. I sat speechless as she walked out the room.

Chapter 10

(Essence)

I decided not to press the subject of what Tanya was doing the night she didn't come home and chalked her behavior up to the fact that she was sheltered as a child and now needed to get out and live a little. Granted, neither one of us had the best childhood. Between the two of us, I had more freedom growing up, and I tried to empathize with Tanya's situation. I loved Tanya and felt we had come too far to let some bullshit come in between us.

There were rumors circulating throughout the club that she was fucking in the back room and had been participating in orgies during private shows. When I asked her about it, she told me the other females were just jealous and the rumors weren't true. I believed her and ignored what was being said until I saw it for myself.

The semester was nearing an end, and I had been studying my ass off and attending class faithfully. I decided playing hooky one day wasn't going to ruin my 4.0 average and opted to stop by Club Delow instead. There was a nice crowd, and the girls were shaking their asses in overtime. I had been in the club for approximately ten minutes but hadn't seen Tanya on stage or in the crowd. I finally decided to ask Shay, the bar manager, about her.

"She did a set earlier," Shay explained. "I haven't seen her since then."

"She left?" I asked.

"I don't think so," Shay said, frowning. "Uh, you might want to check in the back."

"Thanks," I said with a frown and headed toward the door leading to the back room. Mal, Carlos's latest security guard was posted by the door. "What's up, Mal?" I smiled, giving him a friendly hug.

"What's up, sexy?" Mal's light brown eyes travelled from mine down to my low-cut Ed Hardy tee. "You look good."

"Thanks, boo." I was knowingly flirting just enough to get Mal to let me have my way, but not enough to make him feel like I wanted his ass. "Hey, I need to holler at Tan."

Rubbing the dark patch of hair on his chin, Mal scanned

my physique. "I can give her a message," he said, "unless you got another reason for going in." He licked his lips slowly.

"Negative," I said, exhaling. "Real talk, Mal. I just need to holler at my fam." I reached in my pocket and pulled out a crisp one-hundred-dollar bill. *Fuck flirting, I'm growing impatient.* Holding it up, I smiled sweetly.

Mal looked around and then slipped the bill out of my hand and into his pocket. "Don't start no shit," he said. "I just got this job. I ain't trying to lose it."

"I got you, boo."

The back room was dimly lit, smoked out, and reeked of cum and unwashed ass. I felt dirty just entering the place. The room had been partitioned off to make six separate areas. There was a long curtain hanging at the entrance of each makeshift bedroom, but the sides of the curtains were short so anyone passing by could see what was going on behind the curtain. I made it to the fourth curtain and had to clench my teeth to keep from screaming. Tanya was in the room with two brothers. She was butt naked on her knees sucking one of the brother's dick while the other one was hitting her from the back.

The brother drilling her from behind was the first to notice me. "That's what I'm talking 'bout," he said, flashing his gold fronts at me with a sick smile. "Look who came to join us."

The other brother opened his eyes and looked at me. "Hell yeah!" he said, rubbing his hands together. He was so fat I was surprised Tanya could even get to his little bitty penis.

Tanya looked at me with clear wide eyes. "What you doing here?" she asked, wiping her mouth with the back of her hand. She gave me an expression that I hadn't seen since we were kids. She looked innocent and confused.

It was then that I knew bringing her to live with me was a mistake and she had to go.

* * * * *

The sound of the doorbell chiming pulled me from my thoughts. I quickly placed my diary back in the lockbox and stuffed everything back in the drawer. After locking the cabinet and securing the key back in its place under the desk, I headed to the front door. There, I found a box wrapped in shimmery pink wrapping paper, sitting on the welcome mat. There was a white mid-sized delivery van parked by the curve in front of my home. The neon green decal on the side of the van door had the name 'It's In The Basket' in bold letters.

I carried the box in and sat down at the dining room table. I tore open the silver wrapping paper and slid the top off. "What the fuck?" I said, staring at the contents inside.

There was a small brown teddy bear, along with a small note card. I quickly opened the card. My heart felt like it would leap out of my chest as I read the message: 'London Bridge is falling down'. I took a deep breath, trying hard to calm my racing pulse, but it didn't work. There was only one other person alive who would have known the effect those words would have on me.

Chapter 11

(Tatiana)

It was a quarter 'til seven when I arrived at Samuel's office. I hated making the drive, but at least it gave me time to think. Even though it was after business hours, I had a feeling he would still be there. When I saw his Mercedes SLK 300 parked outside in the parking lot, I knew my feeling was right. Samuel was a borderline workaholic. He had several addictions, and work was one of them. It still amazes me that some people can tell others about their issues or problems but can't see their own. They can see your every imperfection but become blind when it's time for them to check themselves.

As my psychiatrist, Samuel had provided me years of therapy, but the truth was, he needed counseling his damn self. I think he used his practice more for dating than he did to help others with their mental instabilities. During the time I was under his care, Samuel and I had crossed the line of doctor-patient confidentiality into doctor-patient sexuality, becoming lovers. In the beginning, when I was emotionally and physically weak, Samuel dominated our love affair. I was brainwashed and completely under his spell. I believed and did whatever he told me. As the years progressed, though, I grew emotionally stronger, and the tables turned completely. The bad girl inside of me resurfaced, and Samuel became the submissive one. I was the master, and he was my slave. I used this to my advantage and finally broke free.

I shook my head and entered the combination on the electronic keypad to open the door. I smiled when the light went from red to green. Samuel provided me the combination to his office back when he thought he and I were going to establish an exclusive relationship. Granted, he had moved on and married since he last saw me, but he hadn't changed his combination, and he knew I had it. *He's been waiting for me,* I thought to myself.

I was glad I had dressed appropriately for the occasion. I wore a jet-black wig that stopped at the curve of my ass, long leather gloves, leather four-inch-heeled boots that caressed my thighs, and a short black trench coat. Underneath the trench coat, my black leather corset and panties stuck to my body like cool cement.

The sounds of Luciano Pavarotti blared through the Bose system inside his office. Samuel never used to play music when he was with a patient, so I hoped this meant he was alone. I slowly opened his office door to find him stretched out on his back on his leather chaise with his eyes closed. He wore a baby blue dress shirt and black slacks. His silk red tie, along with a half-empty bottle of Courvoisier and glass sniffer, were lying on the floor.

Reaching down inside my boot, I gently pulled out the switchblade I had pressed against my thigh. Releasing the blade, I slipped up behind him. Grabbing a handful of his curly locks, I snapped his head back while pressing the sharp steel against the curve of his neck.

His eyes popped open instinctively.

"Did you miss me?" I whispered, flicking my tongue across his earlobe.

"Yes," he whispered, shaking slightly.

Releasing my grip on his hair, I slid in front of him, straddling his lap. Staring into his dark brown eyes, I stroked his face with one hand while continuing to press my blade against his throat with the other.

"You came back," he moaned.

I could feel him growing underneath me, and despite my visit being a business call, it brought me pleasure knowing I still had the same effect on him. "I need your help," I said honestly.

His eyes began to water while he looked at me. "So you only came back for my help?" he said bitterly. "What about what we had?" he asked. "The times we shared? All of this means nothing to you?"

I watched as his tears spilled over the rims of his eyelids and down the curve of his chocolate cheeks. I brushed his tears away with the tips of my fingers and then pulled my hand back, slapping him hard across the face.

He jumped slightly from the hit, causing the knife to scrape his skin.

"Don't act like that," I said sweetly. "Don't play the victim."

Leaning forward, I pressed my lips to his. He opened his mouth, exhaling the scent of cognac. Slowly, his tongue met mine, creating sexual electricity that shot from my lips down to my toes. Pulling back, I looked at him passionately.

"I love you and—"

"I remember," I whispered, cutting him off. "I remember everything."

He looked at me with raised eyebrows. His admission of guilt was written all over his face.

Smiling, I gently slid the knife down his collarbone and then over to where his heart was beating rapidly. "You kept me doped up in a padded room for four years,"

I laughed.

"I…I had to," he stuttered. "The voices in your head…your multiple personalities…they were going to destroy you!"

"Even when facing death, you lie," I said, shaking my head. "Repentance is good for the soul."

"It's true!" he whined. "The life you think was stolen from you wasn't yours. You were living the life of someone else," he continued. "Vicariously. You were delusional!" He attempted to reason with me.

Inside, my anger began to churn slowly. Sliding off his lap, I stood with both feet on the floor, still straddling him. His eyes traveled up my legs to the place where my coat opened. "Did I imagine that?" I asked smugly.

"What?" he asked, trembling.

"The way your eyes traveled my body during every session. I imagined my clit in your mouth?" I asked, as I untied the belt of my coat. I watched as Samuel stared at my breasts hungrily. I slipped the coat off and let it drop it to the floor. "I imagined you fucking me every chance you got?" I asked, tracing my fingers across his neck.

"No," he mumbled lowly. His eyes traveled from my breasts down to my crotchless panties.

The passion etched across his round face caused my pussy to tingle. I was turned on from the shear fact that he both feared and wanted me.

"I fell in love with you," he said, reaching out and grabbing my breast.

Slapping his hand away, I laughed. "Yet you continued to deceive me," I said. I traced the knife down his full lips, staring him in the eyes. I watched as his body began to tense up. "Don't worry." I smiled. "I'm not going to cut out your tongue, Samuel. You're going to need that."

"I wanted to help you," he whispered. "I couldn't stand to see someone so beautiful locked up. You were a prisoner to your own mind."

"Lies," I moaned, swallowing hard.

"It's wasn't real!" he yelled.

"You are a lying bastard," I spat, grasping the handle of the blade tightly. "I should kill you right now."

"Do it!" he said, grabbing my wrist. "If killing me will make you happy, then do it."

"Oh, but death is too easy," I said, lowering the knife. "I believe in reaping what you sow." Stepping away from him slowly, I strutted over to his desk. A large wooden picture frame sat in the corner of the desk, along with a stationery set. Picking up the frame, I stared at the couple standing barefoot on the beach, Samuel with his arm wrapped around a tall, dark-skinned sister wearing a sundress and straw hat. The woman was plus-sized and beautiful. "Wifey is hot," I said, smiling at him. "The two of us could definitely be friends." I said the words sweetly, but it was obvious to me that Samuel caught my threat.

Sitting up, he rubbed his hands together nervously. "What do you want from me?" he asked.

"We'll get to that," I said seductively, "but first I'm going to give you what you want from me." His eyes lit up like a bride's at the altar.

"Come here," I said, sitting down on the edge of the desk. I watched as he slowly walked over, stopping in front of me. I sat the frame back down on the desk, along with the knife. Grabbing him by his shirt, I pulled him close to me. I could feel his heart pounding quickly inside his chest.

Kissing me slowly, he cupped my face in his hands.

"You've been a bad boy, Samuel," I snapped, pulling back. "I think you need to be punished."

"Yes," he moaned.

Raising my hand in the air, I smiled before coming down hard across his face. This time, the impact caused my hand to throb. "On your knees!" I ordered.

On bended knee, Samuel looked up at me like a child kneeling before his parent. Flashbacks of the days I was his patient ran through my mind.

* * * * *

I woke up to an intense pounding inside my head, like someone was beating against the inside of my skull with a two-by-four. I flinched from the pain while looking around the room at my surroundings. The room was empty with the exception of a cushioned stool and the hospital bed I was strapped to. I blinked several times, adjusting my eyes to the rays of light coming through the small window. There were no blinds or curtains at the window, just black metal bars on the outside. My throat was dry and sore, and I swallowed attempting to saturate the intense burning.

He walked through the metal door and stopped when he saw me. He was a handsome man with dark-chocolate-colored skin and curly hair. He adjusted his necktie and slowly walked toward the bed.

"Where am I?" I asked softly.

"You're in the hospital," he said.

"How did I get here?"

"I brought you here," he said, staring at me.

I cleared my throat lightly while trying to make sense of what he was saying. "Can you tell me who I am?" I asked faintly.

He walked closer never taking his eyes off me. "I didn't hear you," he said, frowning. I felt a lump forming in my throat as I broke out in a flood of tears.

"Tell me who I am," I said, practically choking on my own tears. "What's my name?"

"It's okay," he said, rushing to my bedside. "It's okay."

* * * * *

I pushed the thoughts from my mind. Samuel would pay for what he had done, but not at that moment. At that moment, I would reward him with what I knew he wanted the most. Spreading my legs shoulder length apart, I stood over him with my hands on my hips. "Show me how much you missed me," I commanded. Closing my eyes, I arched my back as Samuel ran his tongue up in between my thighs.

Chapter 12

(Essence)

You can't run from your past, no matter how you try to forget there is always someone or something willing to pull you back in. When I ran away to Atlanta, I knew there was a possibility that at any time, the other stiletto could drop, and I would have to face my past and those I walked away from. That day had come. I advised Andrew that I had a meeting arranged with the buyer who had inquired about purchasing my designs, but I was on a quest to stop my drama before it spun out of control.

The drive from Atlanta to Memphis only took me six hours, but riding in silence in my Lexus made it feel like days. My head felt like there were a thousand mini jackhammers drilling inside of it. I practically downed almost a half of bottle of Midol trying to stop the pain, but even that didn't work. I knew the only cure for my pain was peace, and the only way I was going to have peace was by confronting the man I now knew was responsible for my mysterious phone calls and strange gifts. It took me two days to track him down, but those two days felt like two years. Once I finally spoke with him, he agreed to sit down face to face with me so we could finally put an end to his little game.

Staring across the desk, I looked at Samuel. The two of us sat in his office alone. It had been four years since I had seen him, but time had been good to him. He hadn't changed a bit or aged a day. "How did you know where to find me?" I asked.

"Your picture is on the cover of almost every entertainment magazine in the nation," he said.

"Why did you contact me?" I asked.

I watched as he rose from his desk and walked over to the mini bar he had hidden inside his office wall. "Care for a drink?" he asked, looking over his shoulder at me.

"Samuel, this isn't a friendly visit," I reminded him. "I want to know why you have been stalking me."

He took a sip from the half-filled glass and stared at me. "So, now I'm a stalker?"

"Calling me, sending me sick gifts," I said. " Yeah, I would classify that as stalking."

"You're awfully high and damn mighty," he snapped.

"Why shouldn't I be?" I asked. "Against all odds, I managed to make something out of myself."

"Perhaps, but how many people did you hurt to get there?" he asked.

"Are you referring to someone in particular?" I asked.

"What we did was wrong," he said, looking at me as his eyes filled with tears.

"So you suddenly grew a conscience?" I asked, standing. "The man who gets off from counseling the troubled and using their demons against them has a conscience? Where'd you get that from?" I asked, staring at him. "Wifey?"

"Leave my wife out of this!"

"Get your shit together, and I will," I said. "Otherwise, I'll be more than happy to tell her the kind of man she married." I didn't want to destroy Samuel's marriage, but I would if he didn't convince me he could keep our secret until death.

"I've changed," he said, sitting back down.

"Really? So you're no longer sleeping with your patients?" I asked.

There was a pregnant pause between the two of us.

"As I recollect, you wanted me as much as I wanted you."

"Now who needs therapy?" I laughed. "All those degrees," I said, pointing to the wall, "but you lack common sense. It was a game, Samuel—nothing more, nothing less."

He nodded his head and hesitated for a moment before he finally said, "You're right. I shouldn't have contacted you. I shouldn't have sent those things." He wasn't telling me anything I didn't already know.

"Why did you do it then?"

"Seeing you in the paper with your fiance' brought back a flood of memories," he said, walking over to me. "It could have been us. It should have been." Reaching out, he stroked my cheek. His fingers felt cold against my skin.

Pulling away, I frowned at him.

"Everything I did, I did for you," he whispered. "I risked everything for you."

"If sympathy is what you want, you should know me well enough to know you won't get it," I said, standing and facing him. "What you did was to save your ass. Besides, as I remember it, you were compensated accordingly for your assistance," I added.

Samuel walked back over to the wall, this time removing a small wooden panel to reveal a built-in safe. I watched as he removed a thick white envelope and threw it on the desk in front of me. "It's all there," he said angrily, "every damn dollar."

I stared at the envelope and then back at Samuel.

"What do you want me to say, Samuel?" I asked. "What do you want me to do? Tell you I love you?" I asked, standing. "Say that everything you did was for love and that that so-called love was mutual?"

He looked at me and swallowed hard. "Yes," he said somberly.

Smiling sweetly, I touched my fingers to his cheek.

He tilted his head slightly against my palm and closed his eyes. "I could tell you that, Samuel," I said softly, "but you're a shrink. You're trained to decipher through bullshit."

He opened his eyes and took a step away from me.

"So there really is no need for me to lie," I said, lowering my eyes at him. I grabbed my bag and snatched the envelope of his desk. "Don't contact me again," I said, walking to the door. "You won't like it if I have to come back."

"But Tatiana," he said.

"Don't call me that," I snapped, turning to look at him.

"She's alive," he said, sitting down at his desk.

"What are you talking about now?" I was growing tired of his foolishness. It was pathetic. He needed to learn how to let go, and he needed to learn fast. I watched as he pulled the desk drawer out and removed a picture. When he held it out to me, I walked over to the desk and snatched the photo from his hand. My heart felt like it was going to explode at any moment as I stared at the woman in the photograph. Easing down in the chair, I looked at Samuel, hoping my eyes were playing tricks on me.

"She's alive," he said blankly, "and she remembers everything."

Chapter 13

(Tatiana)

Deon had become the thorn that had pierced my ass! When he wasn't constantly calling asking to come by, he was sending me text messages telling me the sex was the bomb. I wanted to tell him to tell me something I didn't know, but I try not to be arrogant. I told him I had a lot on my plate, but he still wouldn't give up. I decided after I handled the situation with my number one enemy, I would find a way to get rid of Deon.

I had provided Samuel with what he needed, and in return, he had given me what I wanted. It was a win-win situation. I would never condone his previous behavior or the role he played during the time I was institutionalized, but I do believe in using everything you have to get what you want. Sometimes that means making deals and arrangements with the enemy.

Running my hands over the front of my dress, I tossed my hair back over my shoulders. I was looking and feeling like new money in my red above-the-knee silk dress. The dress dipped down to my belly button in the front, revealing the curve of my breast. I dimmed the lights in the room and waited patiently for Andrew to arrive. I had invited him to join me at the Embassy for a mini getaway. I told him I wanted no conversation, just straight penetration, and he happily obliged, just as I knew he would. Ten minutes later, there was a knock on the hotel room door.

"Damn." He smiled while staring at me.

Stepping back, I let him into the room. "You like?" I asked, turning slowly on my four-inch heels.

"I love," he said before kissing my lips softly.

Andrew looked sexy as hell in his creased jeans and fitted button-down shirt. I'd forgotten how fine he was, but Spring Training was definitely agreeing with him. "So, to what do I owe this surprise?" he asked.

"Besides the fact that I miss you?" I asked, locking the door. "Nothing, baby."

"I've missed you too," he said, pulling me into his arms.

Snuggling my nose against his neck, I inhaled his scent. "You always smell so good," I whispered, tracing my fingers along his collarbone.

"Not half as good as you."

"If you think I *smell* good, wait until you *feel* me," I said seductively. I planned to show and give Andrew everything he had been missing and then some. I led him by the hand into the bedroom.

"You weren't lying when you said no conversation," he said with a laugh.

"Nope. Tonight is all about body language," I said. "Oh, and phone off. I want no distractions."

Pulling his Blackberry out of his pocket, he nodded. "Yes, ma'am," he said before putting his phone on the nightstand.

I smiled and pushed him down on the bed. Climbing on top of him, I rotated my hips slowly, grinding against his crotch.

"Why are you teasing me?" he asked, breathing heavily.

"I'm just taking my time, baby," I moaned while unbuttoning his pants. "Savoring every inch of you."

"Mmm," he moaned as I stroked his rock-hard stick.

I eased down his body slowly and flicked my tongue across the head of his dick. Reaching over, I pulled out the bag of lemon-honey cough drops I had purchased.

"Boo, do you have a cold?" Andrew asked while watching me.

Slipping one of the lozenges in my mouth, I shook

my head. "Nope," I said before plunging down on his dick.

"Oh, my shh…" he moaned, grabbing a handful of my hair. His body jerked slightly as I continued to suck on his rod.

Turning carefully, I positioned my hips over his face, giving him full access to my lower lips, while holding his throbbing manhood securely with my mouth. "Ohhh," I groaned.

Andrew ran his tongue from my clit up into my wetness and then to the crack of my ass. My body shook as Andrew held my lips open while stroking the inside of my kitty with his hot tongue. Sixty-nine was one of my favorite numbers, and it had never felt so good.

I felt an orgasm approaching at rapid speed. I moved down Andrew's body until I was sitting backwards on his dick. Planting my feet on the bed, I began to rotate my hips slowly. Andrew grabbed my breasts, squeezing them gently. "Harder," I moaned.

He increased the pressure he was applying to my D cups, causing them to sting slightly, but the pain only increased my excitement. I bounced up and down on his stick while clenching the muscles of my pussy. Sitting up, Andrew wrapped his strong arms around my shoulders and gently pushed me over onto the bed. Pulling myself up onto my knees, I arched my back and stretched until my face was pressed down against the bed.

"You feel so good," Andrew whispered as he rotated his hips, grinding deeper into my wet hole.

Bouncing back against him, I looked over my shoulder. "Is it good, baby?" I asked.

"Hell yes," he grunted, squeezing my ass. "You the best, baby—the best."

I smiled as I felt the pressure in me billow out in a wave of warm, sticky wetness.

* * * * *

The next morning, I had to practically push Andrew out the hotel door, and that was after we went for round two. Andrew was handsome, rich, and a good lover, and it was easy to see why she had fallen in love with him. I could have fallen in love with him too. However, after what I had been through, trust was not something I could see myself giving, so Andrew and I being only lovers was probably for the best. I'm a firm believer that when a good man or woman hooks up with someone who has trust issues or any form of insecurity, it leaves them damaged. They are so busy trying to validate or reaffirm their significant other's feelings that eventually they end up with issues themselves. I had enough good left in me not to take Andrew through that, but I was not opposed to giving him the booty!

I had been in awe from the time I drove through the gates of Reynold's Plantation until I pulled into the circular driveway Andrew shared with Essence. The gated community housed 117 holes of golf, four marinas, tournament-ready tennis courts, and mile after mile of shoreline on Lake Oconee. As if that wasn't enough, it was home to the four-star Ritz Carlton Lodge and Spa. The communities and homes were luxurious and breathtaking, and Andrew's home was no exception. Hearing about the home was nothing compared to walking through and experiencing it for myself. From the Grecian columns and crown molding to the marble flooring, the home was five-star. After exploring and searching the bedrooms and baths upstairs, I walked through admiring the accents and décor on the lower level until I came upon the office. Shaking my head, I looked at the drawing table that contained a sketch of an evening gown. I concluded the office belonged to Essence. Walking over to the desk, I pulled on the handles of the mahogany drawers. They were locked securely, just as I suspected. Sitting down, I felt along the bottom of the desk until I found what my fingers were searching for. *Still a simple-minded bitch,* I thought to myself. Opening up the desk, I felt like I had opened Pandora's Box, full of lies and secrets. *Essence really should know better than to bring her dirt home.* After prying open the lockbox, I found the leather-bound diary. I flipped through the pages, barely skimming over the words until I came to the last entry. Reading the random thoughts, I flashed back to the last night I had seen her.

* * * * *

"What are you doing here?" she asked, wiping her mouth with the back of her hand. She gave me an expression I hadn't seen since we were kids. She looked innocent and confused. It was then that I knew bringing her to live with me was a mistake, and she had to go.

"What are you doing?" I asked, staring at her with disgust. "Tan, you got to stop this. Get your clothes on. Let's go."

"Fuck that," the pudgy brother said, grabbing his tiny dick. "We ain't finished yet."

"Damn right," his friend said. "We paid for this pussy, and she can leave when we finished."

I felt my blood pressure rising with every intake of breath. Mal's words echoed in my head: *Don't start no shit.* I guess it was a good thing I hadn't made him any promises. Rushing up to Tanya, I grabbed her arm, attempting to pull her to her feet.

"I'm not going, Tay Tay," she whined, pulling back. She crawled away from us and then pulled her knees up to her chest.

"You heard her, bitch. Step off!" the fatty said, stepping to me.

Looking down, I smiled at the four inches he was working with. Reaching down into my bra, I pulled out my blade and quickly flipped it open.

"Yo, fuck this. These hoes crazy," the other brother, who was obviously the smarter of the two said, stepping into his pants.

"London Bridge is falling down, falling down, falling down," Tanya chanted while rocking back and forth on the floor.

I ignored her chants as I stood toe to toe with the man who, just moments earlier, had his penis in her mouth.

"Marvin, let's bounce." The man was completely dressed and standing outside the curtain.

Marvin looked from me to his friend and then back to me again.

"Stay, Marvin," Tanya moaned, standing on her feet. "We can have fun while the two of them watch." In an instant, Tanya had gone from rocking and singing like a child to a freak.

"Go 'head, Duke." Marvin said. "I'll be on in a minute."

Duke shook his head mumbling, "Crazy-ass nigga," while walking off.

Marvin's eyes shined brightly as Tanya ran her fingers

across his clean shaven head before pressing her lips to his. The sound of the two of them swapping spit made me nauseous.

"Mmm," Tanya moaned.

"Ahhhhhhhhhhh!" Marvin let out a scream that would put a woman to shame. "Stupid bitch!" He fell to his knees, covering his mouth with his hand as blood seeped from the hole Tanya had bitten in his bottom lip.

She looked at me and laughed.

"Stupid ho!" Marvin screamed. He regained his composure and punched her in the face, causing her to crumble to the floor.

It was like I could feel her pain, and her reflex became mine. Before Marvin had the chance to hit Tanya again, I dove in and then out of his roll of fat with my switchblade. He tumbled, falling backwards.

"Ahh!" Marvin cried.

I quickly grabbed Tanya and pulled her to her feet. "Go!" I yelled, pushing her toward the curtain. I quickly grabbed her clothes and started running, dragging her along with me.

"What the hell?" Mal asked as the two of us came bursting out the door.

"Sorry," I breathed. As the crowd outside started to flood the back room, Tanya and I slipped out the side exit and into my car.

* * * * *

"Why do I have to go?" Tanya asked, looking at me. The two of us sat in my Infiniti on our way to Tuscaloosa. After leaving the club, I drove to our apartment and packed our bags as quickly as my energy would allow me and then got right on the interstate. JT had called, explaining that Mal had told him to tell me everything was cool. I didn't know if he meant cool as in 'Marvin's not dead, but the police are looking for your ass' or cool as in 'We handled everything'. I didn't know either way, but I was too tired to care. What I did know and care about was getting Tanya back in therapy.

"It's not working," I explained. "Things are only going to get worse at this rate."

"Is it because everyone loves me?" she asked, staring at me. "That's it, isn't it? You're jealous!" She laughed.

I didn't know which one of her personalities I was speaking to, but whoever she was, she was trying my patience. "No," I said, exhaling. "It's because you're out of control and I don't want you to get hurt."

"Don't worry about me," she snapped. "You need to worry about yourself."

We rode in silence for the remainder of our trip, until Tanya asked me to pull over. "I need to pee," she said.

"But we're almost there," I said.

"Pulling over is the least you can do," she snapped.

"Unless you want me to piss right here on your seat."

I shook my head and pulled into the BP. I sat patiently waiting until she came bouncing out of the store with a smile on her face like she had just won the lotto.

When she opened the passenger door, she handed me a bag. "I got something for you too." She smiled, kissing my cheek.

"Thanks."

"Hey, the tire is really low," she said, shutting the door. "I think there's a nail or something causing a leak."

"Perfect," I grumbled.

* * * * *

The sound of Andrew's cell chirping pulled me from my mental stroll down memory lane. Looking at the screen, I smiled. I was grateful I had snatched Andrew's Blackberry when he wasn't looking. When he called it an hour later looking for it, I advised him I found it underneath the hotel bed. Staring at the screen I read the text message.

Essence: *Hey, baby. Things are going great with the buyers. We hope to have a deal reached by late tomorrow evening or the next day.* Shaking my head I laughed then replied to her message, while pretending to be Andrew.

Andrew: *That's great, baby!*

Essence: *Yep. I'll be in touch as soon as I get a break*

from the meetings.

Andrew: *No problem, boo. Love you!*

Essence: *Love you too!*

Five seconds later, my phone rang. "Hello?"

"I'm waiting," she said before disconnecting the call.

I left Andrew's home, taking a few keepsakes with me. I was headed to my own home, where I could finally come face to face with the woman that betrayed me.

Chapter 14

(Essence)

Staring at the pole, I remembered the days she and I were the Dynamic Duo. It's amazing how bad decisions can turn friends into foes. After informing me he had not handled the task I had assigned him, Samuel provided me with her address and the spare key he kept to her home. According to Samuel, the two of them had developed quite the love affair, and he stayed with her whenever he could find time to visit. I vowed that once I handled her, I would handle him the same way. That way, the two of them could be together in Hell, for all eternity.

The townhome was exactly forty-five minutes away from mine and Andrew's home. I wondered why I never ran into her anywhere. I walked up the winding staircase to the bedroom. Everything was neat and orderly. That's one thing we always had in common: We couldn't stand clutter. I opened the French doors on the closet and pulled down one of the plastic totes. Dropping my bag on the floor, I began to go through the contents of the plastic bin.

Holding up the platinum wig, I flashed back to the night of mine and Andrew's engagement party. The woman who winked her eye at me had looked familiar, and now I knew why. "It was her," I whispered. I pulled the other totes from the shelves, finding nothing but more wigs and hairpieces. In the back corner of the closet was a brown storage box. Sitting down on the floor, I fought back tears as I looked at the contents.

There were pictures of me, Tatiana, and my mother before she passed; pictures of Tatiana and I playing on the playground; and pictures of me, Tatiana, and Vita sitting on the stoop of our old building. There were other pictures of Tatiana as she grew older and even some of her with Samuel. I continued to stare at the photos until I felt a hand on my shoulder.

"Marilyn?"

Wiping the tears from my eyes, I turned and slowly looked over my shoulder. "I'm not Marilyn," I said.

"Essence?" Deon frowned, looking at me. "What are you doing..." He stopped mid-sentence, looking at the wigs and hairpieces on the floor surrounding me.

Standing, I watched him as he processed what he was seeing. "You shouldn't just walk up in other people's cribs," I snapped.

"I. . .I knocked," he said, "and rang the doorbell. There wasn't an answer, but the door was open."

"So you just came in?" I said sarcastically.

"Well, yeah." He cocked his head to the side, looking at me.

"You really shouldn't have done that," I said, shaking my head.

"How do you know Marilyn?" he asked, staring at the pictures I had scattered on the floor. I picked one up and handed it to him as I stood. He looked from the photo to me and then back at the photo again.

"What the fuck?" he asked. "*You're* Marilyn?"

"No. I am."

The sound of her voice commanded both of our attention. As usual, when she entered the room, it lit up. She stood in the doorway of the bedroom, her eyes locked with mine. It had been four years since I had seen her face to face. She had the same stunning cheekbones, the same mesmerizing eyes, and the same make-a-man-drop-to-his-knees physique. It had been four years, but as I looked at her, it was just like looking at myself in the mirror through tainted glass.

Deon looked from one to the other. "Twins?" he said.

"Drew didn't tell me you had a sister," he said, smiling brightly.

"That's because Andrew doesn't know," she said. "There's a lot Andrew doesn't know."

"And he never will," I said, reaching over on the nightstand.

He turned to look at her, preventing him from seeing the iron candlestick holder that landed the blow to his head. We both watched as he dropped face first to the floor.

Chapter 15

(Tatiana)

"Was that necessary?" I asked, looking at Deon's unconscious body.

"He plays in the League with Andrew," she said casually.

That explained why Deon looked so familiar; I had seen him on TV before. "We have to get him some help," I said.

"You really should learn to worry about yourself." She laughed. The laugh that once made me smile no longer had the same effect, the same way the love that I once felt joined us together had grown cold. As we stared at each other, I knew we both wanted the same thing: for the other to be dead. However, unlike Tanya's desire to get rid of me out of jealousy, my desire to rid myself of her was based purely on all she had taken from me.

* * * * *

"Hey, the tire is really low," she said, shutting the door. "I think there's a nail or something causing a leak."

"Perfect," I grumbled. "There's no way we can drive the next hour with a leak."

"Come look at it," she said.

I got out of the car so I could check out the wheel myself.

"Let me get the flashlight out of the trunk," she said, leaving me at the tire alone.

"Tanya, I think it's fine. It may just be the way we parked." I raised my hand to block my eyes from the light she was flashing in my face.

"You really gotta learn to look out for yourself," she said.

I could feel the wind pushing toward my face just before everything went black.

When I came to, I was in Bryce Mental Institution in their medical ward, strapped to a hospital bed. Samuel later explained that I had suffered from a blow to the head and that Tanya had thrown me in the trunk of my car and driven the last hour to Tuscaloosa with the hope that I was dead. When she made it to Bryce, I was still breathing, so she left me with Samuel with the agreement that he would finish me off. Samuel couldn't do it simply because I reminded him too much of Tanya.

Instead, he admitted me to the hospital under an alias. I remained in a coma for a month. When I first came to, I was oblivious to what had happened or how I had gotten there. However, memories slowly began to resurface. When I mentioned them to Samuel, he diagnosed me with multiple personality disorder and started stringing me out on meds. In order to maintain my sanity and regain control, I pretended I believed everything he said. Slowly, he stopped ordering me to take the drugs and had me upgraded from the padded room in the psych ward to a regular private room. This worked out best for Samuel because he now had private access to screw me whenever he wanted to. I stayed in Bryce for four years until Samuel was offered a position in Memphis. In order to keep me close, he had to release me on the basis that I was mentally able to make my own decisions.

"Tell me you'll come with me," he begged.

Smiling, I looked at him. "Of course I will," but as soon as he signed off on my papers, I hauled ass to get away from him.

* * * * *

"When did you decide to take my identity?" I asked, staring at her.

"I didn't take your identity. I just borrowed your memories," she said. "I only flipped things around a little."

"And my designs?"

"I had to have a career," she said with a laugh. "Besides, it wasn't like you were going to be using them anytime soon."

"You had it all planned," I said, shaking my head.

"You just had to come here," Tanya said, looking at me. "It always got to be about Tatiana."

I watched as she twirled the candlestick holder back and forth in between her hands.

"Remember when we were little?" she asked, pacing back and forth across the floor. "You were Savannah's little princess. Whatever Tatiana wanted, it was granted."

"That's because I wasn't acting like a psychotic bitch and throwing tantrums and fits."

Looking at me, she smiled. "Before therapy, that might have actually hurt, but I'm all better now." She winked at me.

"Tell that to him," I snapped. I looked down at Deon, who hadn't moved from his position on the floor.

"He was a victim of circumstance," she said, "much like Savannah."

I felt my heartbeat increasing.

"She once told me you were the good one," she said, exhaling.

"I remember that day," I said, flashing back to the

playground. "It was when you pushed me off the damn tree house. I broke my ankle and ended up wearing a cast for six damn weeks."

"Again, another victim of circumstance," she said. "Remember the night Franklin killed Savannah?" she said, quickly changing the subject.

I didn't answer.

"Remember when I went next door to visit Vita?" she said, smiling. "I called Franklin at the church that night."

"You're lying!"

"Nope, I really did," she said in a childlike voice. "I told him Mommy was in the bedroom with a strange man and I couldn't get her to open the door. I had no idea he was going to go postal." She laughed. "But shit happens, you know?"

I took a deep breath, trying to maintain my composure. "Which one of you did it?" I asked.

"One of who?"

"Samuel told me about the many voices running around in your head," I said, stepping toward her.

"Let's see," I began, "there was Mimi, Lisa, and Clarissa. Clarissa was a bitch." I laughed. "She was also a ho. That was the back room favorite at Delow," I said, standing with my hand on my hip.

"You don't know what you're talking about," she

said lowly.

"You thought that was all you?" I asked, giggling. "Bitch, please. You're certifiable, and just as soon as the wrong thing sets you off, Andrew is going to know your ass is crazy."

"Shut the fuck up!" she screamed.

"Speaking of Andrew," I said, "he's a keeper."

She looked at me and frowned.

"Oh yeah, we met," I said, licking my lips. "Best sex he ever had."

"You lying bitch!" she yelled. "Andrew wouldn't touch you!"

"Oh, but he did." I gave her a small smirk. "He touched me in more ways than one." The truth was, Andrew believed I was her. That's why he never questioned my asking for his spare key to their home. I told him I left mine in another purse, and he fell for it.

"You're lying!"

"Call him and ask him," I suggested. I waited as she dialed his number. The phone in my jean pocket began to ring loudly, I pulled Andrew's Blackberry from my pocket and held it up. "It's for you." I smiled.

Chapter 16

(Essence / Tanya)

It wasn't that I didn't love my sister. She had been my childhood best friend. However, I always felt like I was competing for attention whenever she was around. We both had the looks, but she had the personality to go with it. Whether it was making friends in school or charming out mother's men, she stood out, and this bothered me. Tatiana was my only real friend and my biggest competition, so I created imaginary playmates, making myself the popular one and the leader. They spoke to me and listened to what I had to say—at least until Clarissa came along. She was the strong one and the most rebellious. The two of us were sitting in the living room reading when William came to see Mama. Tatiana was sitting on the couch watching TV. I remember William coming in with a brand new drawing pad for Tatiana and a damn candy bar for me.

"I know how much you like to sketch," he said to her, "and they had them on clearance."

"Thanks!" Tatiana said, grinning from ear to ear.

"She'll always be number one," Clarissa whispered to me.

I nodded my head in agreement.

I remember after Franklin came and committed the murders, I felt an enormous hole in my heart, and my mind was jumbled with my own thoughts. I had just returned from Vita's when I heard the shots and Tatiana's scream. I can still remember the stench that came along with death as I walked down the hall to the bloody crime scene.

"Why did he come?" Tatiana whimpered. "He never comes on Wednesday. Never."

I remember our neighbors rushing in to see what the commotion was all about. As I slipped in the kitchen to get the knife, none of them noticed. It was Tatiana who found me hiding in my closet, struggling for air and with blood running down my arms from me slicing both my wrists open.

During the time I was recovering from my wounds in the hospital, I didn't get to see Tatiana. I remember Clarissa and I got so angry that when the nurse came to draw our blood, we snatched the needle off the tray and jammed her in the hand with it. They restrained me to the bed until the doctors ordered I could be released. Tatiana was already in Angel's House, but when it came time for my placement, the court ordered a mental evaluation. After counseling sessions and several tests, they sent me to Bryce, where I spent seven years of my life. I would have still been there if it hadn't been for Samuel. Samuel became my counselor after my seventeenth birthday and my lover before I hit eighteen. I never wanted Samuel, but I knew if I was ever going to live free, I needed someone inside the facility on my team. He was the one who helped me find Tatiana.

Life was good at first, but the voices kept coming back to me. Clarissa was the ring leader. She had me convinced that Tatiana was Delow's star because she was doing more than just climbing a pole and shaking it. "We can take her spot," she said. "It's okay to be extra friendly with the patrons, as long as they're paying."

I remembered the game my mother use to play with her friends, and Clarissa convinced me this would make me just like her, so I did it. I sucked and screwed man after man, until Tatiana came to my rescue again. As I think about it now, she was always the one saving me from something.

Walking over to the place where I had been sitting

on the floor, I grabbed my bag. As I pulled out the gun, I wondered why no matter what I did, she still loved and forgave me. "Promise me one thing," I said, cocking the gun.

She stared at me with wide, beautiful eyes. "What's that?"

"You'll always love and remember me," I said sadly.

"Yes."

I smiled at her as I raised the gun and pulled the trigger, releasing two shots into her chest.

Chapter 17

(Essence/ Tanya)

I was grateful I made it home before Andrew. I needed to take a long, hot bath and burn everything I was wearing. I strolled through the foyer, dropping my keys and bag on the table. I was happy to be home, but something didn't feel right. Stepping into my office, I wanted to scream. My desk was unlocked, and the drawers were open and empty. The designs I had hidden in the desk were gone, along with my money and Tatiana's diary. She snatched everything! I had no idea what she planned to do with it, but it didn't matter now that she was dead. I slammed the drawers shut. I would tell Andrew I was no longer interested in design. In fact, maybe being a housewife wasn't so bad after all. I had endured my share of excitement, and I was ready for boring.

I had just finished a luxurious soak when the doorbell rang. Slipping into my silk kimono, I strolled to the door. "Hello," I smiled.

The man was dark-skinned and pretty. There was something about him that looked familiar to me. He wore a dark blue uniform with a white patch that said 'A-1 Automotive'. I wondered if Andrew had reported a problem with one of the vehicles.

"What can I do for you?"

Pop! Pop! Pop!

All I felt was breathtaking pain as everything faded to black.

Epilogue

(Essence)

I looked out the window of the Delta 745 and exhaled. Andrew and I were finally taking the trip to Milan that he had promised me. It had been nine months since Barron came to my door and opened fire. I had forgotten about Barron before that; after all, it had been two years. I never would have expected him to turn stalker, but I guess that's why you shouldn't play with other people's emotions.

As it turns out, Barron had been stalking for months. He was the one behind the phone calls and the crazy gifts that I wrongly accused Samuel of. When the police apprehended him, he was in a hotel room staring at the TV with our sex tape playing.

I stayed in ICU for four days before my condition improved and I was put in a regular room. Andrew stayed by my side the entire time. I was thankful that, with the exception of my scars, I had no permanent damage from the shooting.

"Babe, did you see this headline?" Andrew asked, handing the paper to me.

"Is this ever going to die down?" I asked, shaking my head. We had made the front page again: *Essence Monroe says she forgives her twin.*

"Babe, you got to admit, the story is interesting," he said, flashing his eyes at me. "Two girls separated as children, one on the road to success, and the other snaps to crazy and tries to take her spot. It's like something out the movies," he laughed.

"I'm just glad you stuck by me," I said.

When I finally came out of ICU, I was able to tell Andrew the story of my life. To my surprise, he didn't run in the other direction. He said he loved me no matter what, and he was staying. That kind of love and devotion earns a man your trust!

"Just think, boo," he said, "I still can't believe she was going to trick me into believing she was you."

"I know," I said. "It's scary."

"Like I don't know my own baby," he laughed, shaking his head.

"I know. Right," I said.

"I'm just glad Deon came to and got you help in time,"

he said, stroking my cheek. "I can't imagine not having you in my life."

"I guess it's a good thing you'll never have to deal with that," I said with a smile. I stood, excusing myself to the bathroom.

I said I told Andrew my life story, and I did. I just left out the parts that I didn't want him to know. Things like his real fiancee' was the one who was carried out in a body bag at what is now 'our' home. Those kinds of things. To my relief, Deon believed Tanya was Marilyn, the one with whom he had the one-night stand. However, every once in a while, when the team's families got together, I would catch him giving me the suspicious eye.

I destroyed the diary Tanya had used to turn my life into hers. I no longer needed to keep a record of those memories because Andrew and I were about to make a whole lot of new ones.

As for Samuel, I told him he would reap what he sowed, and he was reaping it well. There was an anonymous tip made to the Memphis DA from Malcolm, courtesy of me, advising them of Samuel's sordid relationships with his ill and vulnerable patients. After a thorough investigation, he was indicted and charged for malpractice. The reports say some of his patients were as young as fourteen.

I would miss Tanya, but the feeling was bittersweet. On the one hand, we were blood, and you can never forget your family. I wanted her dead, but I never actually had any intention of killing her. On the other hand, she tried to kill me twice! Some shit is just unforgiveable.

It's a good thing that survival is in my nature.

Knock. Knock.

I opened the bathroom door and pulled Andrew into the small lavatory. I was about to introduce him to the Mile High Club properly. Dropping to my knees, I unzipped his jeans and pulled out his magic stick that was already halfway ready for me. I told you, it's in my nature to survive. But the good thing for Andrew is that it's also in my nature to be bad.

Enjoy a bonus read

from

Mz. Robinson

CHAPTER 1

"I'm sorry, baby," Kenny said, kissing my forehead. "I promise it'll be just the two of us next weekend.

"You've been saying that for the last month," I said annoyed.

"What am I suppose to do, Shontay?"

Stepping back, I put some distance between the two of us. "Why don't you try telling Alicia that we've had Kiya for the last four weekends, and this weekend, we'd like to spend some time alone?"

Frowning, Kenny rubbed his hand back and forth across the stubble on his face. "Alicia is trying to get her cosmetology license," he said. "She works through the week, so that only leaves the weekends for her to go to classes."

I couldn't believe my ears. Not only was he canceling our plans for another Saturday alone, but he also wanted me to support his ghetto-tramp baby's mama in her educational endeavors. I had put my own education on hold to support him and our marriage, and not once did I get a thank you. Now he had the audacity to support Alicia's trifling ass.

"Maybe she should have thought about that before she decided to lay up with someone else's man," I snapped. "Besides, I thought you told me Kiya was going to be with her grandmother this weekend."

"She was, but Alicia's mom decided to go to Tunica," he said.

"She didn't tell Alicia until this morning."

Rolling my eyes, I threw my hands up in frustration. I was defeated, and arguing about the subject wasn't going to change a thing. Sitting down on the edge of the bed, I exhaled. "I'll think of something for the three of us to do together," I said.

"Thanks, baby," he said smiling.

***

Scanning over the selection of paperback and hardcover books, I searched for something to take home and read. I was spending a beautiful Saturday afternoon in Barnes and Nobles alone. After thirty minutes with Kenny and Kiya, I decided I needed a break. I pulled out a paperback titled G-Spot by Noire, and began to read the back cover.

"That's a hot piece," I heard someone say.

I looked up and found myself staring into a pair of gray cat-like eyes. The eyes complimented thick eyebrows and a pair of succulent-full lips. The man they belonged to had smooth, flawless skin, the color of pecans. I nonchalantly lowered my eyes, and glanced over his wide built frame. Even in the dirt-covered overalls he was wearing, I could tell he had large biceps and an athletic physique. He was wearing a dingy black bandana that hid his hair, and cement covered leather steel toe boots. Sexy, even covered in dirt, I thought. I redirected my attention back to his eyes, and asked, "Excuse me?"

He smiled, revealing a set of straight white teeth. "G-Spot," he said. His voice was deep and sexy. He had the type of voice that was perfect for phone sex. "It's a hot piece," he said. His thick tongue rolled along the edge of his bottom lip, causing heat to surge through the seat of my panties.

I shifted my weight from one leg to the other, and asked, "You've read it?" His eyes traveled from my face down to my low cut tank top, then back up again. "Yes," he said, "it's one of my favorites."

"Thanks." I said, giving him a small smile. As I turned around to walk away, I could feel his eyes burning a hole in my ass through my denim Capri pants.

"So, you're just going to take my suggestion and run?" he asked.

I turned around slowly, and my eyes locked with his. There was something so sexual about the way he looked at me. For a brief second I could have sworn I saw "Let's fuck", spelled out in his corneas.

"You could at least tell me your name," he said seductively.

Trying to control the flutters in my stomach, and keep my hardened nipples from poking a hole in my shirt, I crossed my arms across my breasts.

"Thanks again," I said, instead of telling him my name. "Have a nice day."

I quickly walked up the aisle to the checkout. I was practically running to get away from him, not because I thought he was a psycho or a rapist. But because, in less than five minutes, he had accomplished what my husband hadn't been able to do in weeks; he managed to make my pussy wet.

After making my purchase, I sat in my car watching the front doors of the store. After five minutes, he walked out carrying a large bag. He walked with his head held high, and this air of confidence. The brother was fine. I'm talking fine with a capital F, as in "fuck me fine". I stalked him until he climbed into a white Ford F150 with SB Building & Construction painted in bright red letters on the door, started the engine, and pulled out of the parking lot.

I reclined the driver's seat of my Honda Accord and unbuttoned the top of my pants. The dark tint on my windows prevented anyone from seeing inside. That was a good thing, because I sat there in broad daylight with my AC blowing and my fingers inside my panties, stroking my throbbing clit. I closed my eyes, and a vivid picture of the stranger filled my head. I massaged and played with my clit until I came. The entire time I had been daydreaming that he was down on his knees with his face in between my legs.

***

I walked through the doorway of my home and cursed. My living room was a mess. "Damnit," I muttered under my breath.

I tripped over a bikini clad black Barbie, and kicked the doll across the floor. I looked around the room. There were dolls and building blocks everywhere. The room looked like a toy factory.

Why can't he make her pick-up after herself?

Kicking my way through the toys to the kitchen, I contemplated on cleaning up my stepdaughter's mess, but then decided against it. I had been playing Kenny's maid for the last eight years, I was not about to do the same for his daughter.

Before Kenny and I got married two years ago, we had dated for six years. He was the first man I ever trusted; that's where I made my mistake. I thought he could do no wrong. I put his ass on a pedestal, and damn near kissed the ground he walked on. In return, he made a fool of me by running from motel to motel with woman after woman after woman. It's not that Kenny isn't a good man; he just has a big problem keeping his dick to himself.

He cheated more times than I can count, and probably more than I care to know. Before we got married, there were several occasions my best friend and I busted him with other women. It was never a difficult task to catch Kenny, because he was never good at covering his tracks.

Whenever there was a new female in his life, he would start acting real shady. He'd come in at the wee hours in the morning, stumbling over his explanation of where he was and what he had been doing. He even walked around the house with his cell phone, like it was glued to his hip. If he went into the kitchen to get a glass of water, he carried his cell. When he got up to change the TV, he had his cell. Even when he went into the bathroom to take a piss, he had that damn phone. Kenny carried his phone around like it was his second dick. So, it was quite obvious when he was cheating on me.

I have to give him some credit; he managed to keep his daughter a secret for the two years of our marriage. I found out about Kiya, courtesy of three-way calling. To make a long story short, I checked his cell phone call history online, and discovered he had been calling this one particular number several times a day. I had my girl, Octavia, call the number on three-way, and the two of us were greeted by the sweet voice of a little girl. When her father took the phone from her, his voice sent my heart straight to my toes. The little girl was Kiya Janai Green, and her father was my husband.

I kicked Kenny out of our home that day. I was hurt beyond words. Looking back now, I don't know if my heart felt more pain from his keeping his daughter a secret from me, or more so because another woman had given him the one thing I couldn't. My right to conceive and bare children was stolen from me at an early age.

Anyway, after two weeks of Kenny begging to come home, and my suffering through unbearable loneliness, I let him move back in. I swallowed what little pride I had left, and agreed to try and make our extended family work.

The sound of the door unlocking caught my attention. I sighed loudly, preparing myself for Kiya to come running into the room.

"Hey baby," Kenny said, walking through the doorway alone. He pulled out the chair next to me and sat down.

"Where's Kiya?" I asked.

"I took her to my mom's crib," Kenny said.

"How is Etta?"

"Good," he said smiling. "She asked about you."

I gave him my "yeah right" look, and rolled my eyes. Kenny's mother had no love for me whatsoever. I overheard her telling him once that I was holding him back. Imagine that. I have my Bachelor's in Elementary Education, a decent job as Assistant Director at a daycare, and good credit. Kenny worked for the City of Huntsville cutting grass, only had his GED because I helped him study for the exam, and he couldn't get a glass of water on credit without me co-signing. He wasn't even providing a roof over my head. The house we lived in also belonged to me.

My grandmother, Martha, God rest her beautiful soul, bought the three bedroom house for me before she died. To top it off, the 2000 Mitsubishi Eclipse he drove was in my name. Etta either had too much faith in her son, or she was plain delusional. I was not holding her son back, I was carrying his ass.

"I'm serious, she asked about you," he said unconvincingly.

I studied his facial features, while pretending to listen to him ramble on and on about Etta's garden. I loved Kenny, but he had nothing on the brother from the bookstore.

Kenny is dark skinned, with high cheekbones and wide dark eyes. He isn't what most women would consider handsome, but he oozes with self-confidence.

His self-confidence gave him a certain sex appeal.

I stood up, leaned over and kissed his lips. I parted his lips with my tongue, while running my fingers through the low-cut waves in his hair. Standing up, he placed both of his hands on my ass. "How you feeling?" he asked, in between kisses. That was his way of asking if I wanted to make love. I grabbed the hardness in his pants, and gave it a gentle squeeze. "Give me five minutes to start the shower." I said seductively. "I'll be waiting," he said, rubbing his hands up and down my backside.

***

Ten minutes later, I stood wrapped in a thick terry cloth bath towel. I was dripping wet from my warm shower, the shower I had anticipated on sharing with my husband. I walked into the bedroom and looked at him, as disappointment ran through my body. Kenny was stretched out across the bed, sleeping like a newborn baby.

He slept for the rest of the night, so I crawled up with my new book, and ended up reading it from beginning to end. The brother from the store was right, it was a hot piece. In fact, it was so hot that my fingers were deep inside my pussy, while Kenny lay beside me snoring.

Prologue

Here I am alone on a Friday night. I'm tempted to pick up the phone and call Tony for a little one on one personal attention. Tony is my call whenever I want some brother. He knows there could never be anything between us but sex and he accepts it. I educated him on my "no strings policy", the first day we met and he's been "on call" for me every since.

I'm not like most women; I don't need a full-time man to validate who I am. I'm educated, independent, and sexy. The only time or place I have for a man is in my bed because no matter how independent and strong I may be, the fact still remains that I can't fuck myself so I dial the digits..

"Hello."

"Are you busy?" I ask, getting right to the point.

"What's up?" He responds, knowing exactly what I'm calling for, but playing his little game anyway.

"Answer the question," I said. "Are you busy?"

"Depends on what's up." You see this is how a brother messes up the groove, asking a lot of stupid questions.

"Are you busy or not?" I ask, impatiently.

Sighing, he said, "No, I'm chillin' over my home boy's house."

"Oh, well you're busy so I will let you go."

"What you doing tonight?" He asks, in a low, sexy voice, and I know he's on the hook.

"I don't know, there's no telling," I said. So what if I'm lying he doesn't know that. I could have something real important to do tonight.

"Can I come over?" He asks.

Yeah, that's what I'm talking about! I hesitate shortly then say,

"What time you talking about?"

"Like in thirty minutes?" Tony responds.

"Give me an hour and a half - I have to run an errand." I have nothing to do but I want to at least take another quick shower. It's like a pre-sex ritual for me.

"That's fine," He said. "I need to run by the drug store anyhow. I'll see you in a few."

The good thing about Tony is he always wears a condom. I don't have to ask or anything, he takes the initiative and I am quite grateful. The last thing I want to do is to have to put him out my house because he refused to strap up. I want some but not that bad, if a man does not want to wear protection I can do without. There are enough women in this world with unwanted babies and incurable diseases because they got caught up in the moment. I'm not trying to be anybody's Baby Mama nor am I trying to be another statistic. It's simple to me: no condom equals no sex!

After I hang up I take a quick shower, spray on my Very Sexy by Victoria Secret and slip into my black lace see thru nightgown. I think if you are going to do it; you might as well do it right. So I lit my vanilla aromatherapy candles and popped the Isley Brothers CD in the stereo. About thirty minutes later, Tony arrives dressed in jeans and a blue striped Polo shirt.

Tony is a light-skinned brother, about 5'9' with a low cut fade and a little on the slim side. The brother could definitely use a few home-cooked meals, but he won't get them here.

"I see you got the mood set," He said, stepping through the front door.

Giving him a small smirk, I shut the door behind him. The ambiance is for me, not for him. Tony is cool but he's not working with the biggest jewel there is, so I need all the help I can get to experience the Big O.

"Damn you look good!" He says, as he turns to face me with a big stupid grin.

Smiling, I make my way to the bedroom. I don't want conversation, just straight action. I want him to do what he came to do then hit the road so I can get me some rest. Following me down the hall, Tony began stripping down to his briefs. Slipping the straps of my nightgown off my shoulders, I let it slip down around my ankles. I had no panties to remove because I wasn't wearing any. Stretching out across my satin sheets, I closed my eyes before Tony can say anything, then I spread my legs wide. He knew what I wanted immediately and showed it when he ran his tongue up in between my thighs. This is definitely one thing he's good at. Grabbing his head, I pushed it farther in between my thighs until his lips were buried deep in between mine. Tony rotates his tongue inside of me slowly and smoothly, as he stirs my wetness with his tongue. He moves from my pussy to my clit and back down to my pussy, causing a wave of heat to surge through my northern region. Tony eats my pussy until he's out of breath and the insides of my thighs are sticky from my warm cream.

I opened my eyes and smiled, letting him know I'm content with his oral performance. I got mine and at that moment that was all that was important, that and the fact that he's sliding the condom over his erection right at this very moment. Tony enters me slow and easy. I don't know why, because although I keep my coochie tight, sex with him is like throw- ing a wrench in a toolbox. Nonetheless Tony is taking his time moving in and out of my warmth, until finally his leg starts to shake and he begins to moan my name.

"Ugggghhhhhhh."

It's over. His job here is done.

The next morning I woke up feeling good and somewhat satisfied. Un-like a lot of women, I am content with a man only coming over for a booty call. What is the big deal? I get some of my needs taken care of and he gets to bust a nut. It's a win - win situation. I know there are some good men in the world whom are relationship worthy. I just don't know any personally. Besides knowing what I know about men, there is no possible way I'll give one the chance to break my heart. It's my personal philosophy that a man can't break your heart if you never let him in it.

My first and only heartbreak came on a cold frosty night in Decem- ber, 1987. It was two a.m. and I was lying in my bed with my eyes wide open staring into thc darkness.

"Where have you been all day?" I hear mama ask in a strong tone. My parents were in the kitchen having another argument. "Don't start Charlene," Daddy said.

I could hear the sound of dishes clanking. Daddy was re-heating the dinner Mama had made for us the night before.

"Don't start?" She asked, loudly, just like a dozen times before, but something told me that this argument was going to be different.

"You walk in this house at two a.m. and you have the audacity to tell me don't start?"

Ding. I hear the microwave timer go off.

"Let me tell you one fucking thing," She continued.

I propped myself up on my elbows. I couldn't believe my ears! I had never heard my mother curse before. She never so much as used the word Hell out of context.

"I'm not going to continue to put up with your bullshit, Charles," She said.

"I'm tired Charlene and I don't want to hear this shit." I could hear daddy open and close the microwave and pull open the silverware drawer.

"You're tired?" Mama was practically screaming, "No, Charles! I'm tired! I'm tired of you coming in here all hours of the morning smelling of liquor and that bitch's cheap perfume!"

What bitch? I was tempted to run my nosey little ass in the kitchen and ask.

"You don't know what the fuck you're talking about, Charlene," Daddy said.

I could hear one of our rickety kitchen chairs squeak. Someone had sat down.

"I found the picture of Cheryl Ann in your wallet," She said.

That ugly old woman? I asked myself. Cheryl Ann was the neighborhood bootlegger. She had to be at least fifty and she didn't hold a candle to my mother. My mother was a walking mold of brown sugar, smooth sweet and thick. My mother had and still has to this very day what you call an hour glass figure. Cheryl Ann reminded me of the wicked witch from the Wizard of Oz. She had this long nose and at the tip was a hairy black mole. What my father wanted with her, I'll never know. Going from my mother to Cheryl Ann was without a doubt, like going from sugar to shit. Even at the tender age of 10 I knew I was fine because everyone told me I was the miniature version of my mother. The only thing she didn't have that I did was my honey brown eyes and curly jet-black hair. I had to give thanks to my father for those.

"Oh, so now you going through my things? Charlene, you trippin'. And you better settle down before you wake my baby," He said.

"Were you thinking about your baby when you were laying on top of that nasty ass bitch?"

My mother lowered her voice. There was brief silence then I heard the sound of glass shattering across the floor.

"Woman, what in the hell is your problem?" Daddy screamed.

"You are my problem!" She yelled, "You and your ugly ass whore!"

"Well I can fix that."

I heard the chair go across the floor again. Then there were footsteps coming up the hallway. I knew it was my father because they were loud. Daddy always walked hard. He was going into their bedroom. I knew when I heard their closet door swing open, he was packing his bags. I lay back in my bed and pulled my covers tightly up around my neck as a cascade of tears ran down my cheeks. I hadn't heard Mama say a word as our front door slammed closed behind him but I knew she was standing or sitting in that kitchen crying too.

I watched Mama cry what seemed to be at least a hundred times before and since that day. She did everything for my father except wipe his ass. How did he show his gratitude? By cheating with the ugliest woman in the neigh- borhood and then sending her divorce papers by mail. Don't get me wrong; I love my father deeply. To this day we still have a relationship. I just can't get over the fact that he chose ugly ass Cheryl Ann over his family.

I've also chosen not to get caught up based on the drama my best friend Shontay has had with her husband Kenny. She has been with Kenny for at least six years and she's caught him with numerous females in their car or at some ran down motel. The majority of his cheating came before their marriage but I'm prone to think once a cheater always a cheater. I hate to sound cliché but it's been said time and time again: You can't teach an old dog, new tricks. I agree, especially if that dog walks upright on two legs and thinks with his dick.

I promised myself after my daddy left that I would never let a man get close enough to bring me to tears. So when I was old enough to date I set a guideline that I wouldn't keep a man longer than a year. This wasn't a big issue back then because it was high school and most relationships didn't last longer than six months. When I got to college I had to change my game plan. I wasn't dealing with immature high school students anymore; I was dealing with immature high school graduates. So my policy changed from not keeping a man for longer than a year to not having a man at all.

From my freshman year at Spelman College up until now I've had nothing more than homey -lover friends and that's exactly how I like it. I'll go out with a man, and if we have sexual chemistry, we became sex partners. I think it's the perfect arrangement and most of the men I meet think so, too but occasionally, I'll meet a man who can't stick with my "no strings attached" policy.

I'll never forget Thomas. I met him my junior year at Spelman College and he was a senior at Morehouse. We went out a couple of times; had a one night rendezvous. He graduated and I never heard from him again.

Two years later after I had moved back home to Alabama and was on my way to starting my own business, I got a phone call from Thomas. I was surprised that he knew how to locate me. I don't know why, considering I still had the same cell phone number I had in college. Anyway, Thomas explained that he was in town on business and that it would be good to see me again. I agreed, and the two of us met up for dinner that same night. Thomas was still the light skinned cutie I remembered. We talked and had a few drinks then ended up back at his hotel. For the entire week he was in town, we went out and had a good time, that ended back at the hotel for an even better time. The day he left for Denver, we promised to keep in touch. You know the whole "If you're ever in Denver, call me" and the "If you're ever in Huntsville, call me." People say it all the time but mostly because they have nothing else to say to you and they're just trying to be polite. Thomas didn't see it that way because the next thing I know he's in Huntsville every weekend and he's calling me. After a month, he finally asked me where our relationship was going.

"I didn't know we were in a relationship," I said.

"I just assumed after everything that's been happening, we were committed," He said, frowning.

"Thomas, I'm not looking for a man."

"Well, what am I?" He asked.

"A friend," I responded, and this is when things got a little ugly.

"A friend?" He asked, grimacing," I left my wife for you and now you're telling me I'm a friend."

The peculiar thing about this whole mess was that I didn't know his ass was married. There was no wedding ring or even any discoloration on his finger to indicate he had been wearing one. When I asked him about what he had been doing since college it would have been nice if he had told me he got married.

"Your wife," I said, cutting my eyes at him," I didn't know you were married."

"You didn't ask!"

He had a point but I was not about to be blamed for his mistakes.

"Well you should have asked if I wanted a commitment before your dumb ass left your wife," I snapped.

The conversation got worse with every word. It finally ended with him yelling "Fuck you!" as I stormed out of his hotel room.

That was the last time I saw Thomas. After that, I changed my cell number for the first of five times. There would be four more brothers who couldn't adhere to the rules. Each of them gave me the: "I want to take this to the next level" speech. Each of them received the: "This is the only level I want us to go to" speech. Even though there were a couple of good prospects out of the four- I wasn't trying to pursue anything serious. I had my mind made up that even when a man asked to see you exclusively; he still has his share of on the side booty waiting in the rafters.

Get your copy of the Love, Lies & Lust series today!

PRESENTS

G&L Enterprises is the biggest marketing firm in the country. Each year thousands of intern applicants apply with the hope of securing a position with the illustrious firm. Out of a sea of applicants, Asia is bestowed the honor of receiving an internship with G&L. Asia is beautiful, ambitious, and determined to climb her way up the corporate ladder by any means necessary. From crossing out all in her path, to seducing Parker Bryant the CEO of G&L, Asia secures a permanent position with the marketing giant. However, her passion for success will not allow her to settle for second best. Asia wants the number one spot, and she'll stop at nothing, including betraying the man responsible for her success to get it. Asia, is taking corporate takeover to a whole new level!

August 2011

Lies, deceit and murder ran rampant throughout the city of Atlanta. Real and his lady, Constance, were living in the lap of luxury, with fancy cars, expensive clothes and a million dollar home until someone close to them alerted the feds to their illegal activity.

At the blink of an eye their perfect life was turned upside down. Just as Real was sorting things out on the home front, the head of Miami's most powerful Cartel gave him an ultimatum that would eventually force him back into the life he had swore off forever. Knowing this lifestyle would surely put Constance in danger, he made plans to send her away until the score was settled but things spiraled out of control. Now Real and Constance are in a fight for survival where friends become enemies and murder is essential. Atlanta's underworld to Miami's most affluent community—no stone was left unturned as Real fought to keep Constance safe while attempting to regain control of the lifestyle he once would kill for.

From the city of Atlanta to the cell block of Georgia's most dangerous prison, life under the City Lights would never be the same.

August 2011

Young Hollywood, the youngest goon of a notorious rich clique from Hollywood Court projects is destined to make his name known throughout the entire Westside of Atlanta. Certified and ruthless, Young Hollywood is worth a half a million before the age of sixteen, and is well on his way until tragedy strikes. Young Hollywood's home is invaded, and his son is held for ransom. Violated, blood thirsty and reckless, he vows for revenge as he combs the city for answers.

Once inside the Georgia Penal System, Young Hollywood continues on his ruthless traits until he is placed on high max with hardened criminals. There, Young Hollywood meets up with a man he never knew before. After they untie, the real A-Town Veteran is released from prison after serving twenty straight years, but not before sucking up every piece of game and knowledge he could.

This entertaining triumph goes from the streets, to the prison system and to the corporate world of record labels and rap entertainment. This highly anticipated, descriptive urban novel about crime, corruption and passion in Atlanta's own underworld will have you on your toes from the first page to the very last. This is one masterpiece you'll never want to end.

August 2011

The King, raised in the hood with his family, saw a lot of suffering. He witnessed death and destruction within his own family—poverty and desperation of his own people. Instead of being part of the problem, he became part of the solution and rose to the top of his game. In his mind…it was survival.

After an encounter with a brilliant scientist, King began to plot something so huge, that no one would see it coming or be able to stop the cycle…not even the police.

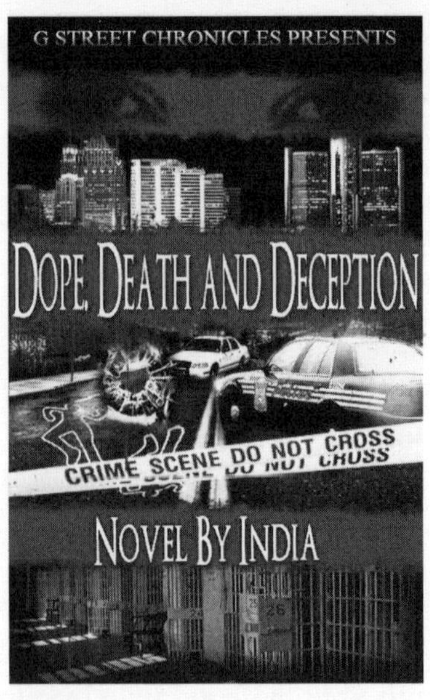

Meet Lovely Brown, a 20 year old from Detroit, MI that has witnessed too much! After her father was sentenced to major time behind bars her mother turns to drugs and is later found dead because of it. She is left to take care of her younger sister after her older sister bails! She's been homeless and hungry, taking various street jobs to put food on the table for her baby sister Tori, but after a case of mistaken identity Lovely is left all alone with no family because they've all become victims of the streets, in one way or another. She vows to take vengeance into her own hands and shut down the dope game by becoming one of it's major players, operating under the name LB. Everything was running smoothly until she finds out that she has a 1 MILLION dollar bounty placed on her head and seemingly overnight everything begins to fall apart. In the mist of her chaos she falls in love with a guy that she knows little about. They've both been keeping secrets but his could prove to be deadly for her! Immediately she thinks of an exit strategy but will she make it out the game alive?

October 2011

Highly Anticipated Sequel to Dope Death and Deception

Lovely Brown was living the good life as Detroit's top drug dealer, operating under the alias LB. Everything was going smooth until her father Lucifer escaped from prison, ready to return to the throne and destroy anyone in his path, including Lovely. While running for her life, she was also being investigated by the Feds and simultaneously set-up for the murder of her mafia connects' nephew. This resulted in a ONE MILLION DOLLAR bounty being placed on her head. Achieving the impossible, Lovely managed to escape unscathed.

Now, five years after she left all the Dope, Death and Deception behind and she's finally living a normal life, things get complicated. Issues from her past come right to her front door. Once again Lovely finds herself in a bad situation with her back against the wall—looking sideways at everyone in her corner. Lies have been told and love has been tested.

Just when she thought things were over, it looks as if someone is Still Deceiving!

Trapped in time, Jay is a prisoner of his own mind. A victim of multiple personalities, Jay and his alter ego Capo are two very different men sharing one body. Jay is a laid back man who has grown tired of the streets and doing his cousin Ant's dirty work. Although, those close to Jay have grown to love and accept both of his personalities, he longs to gain control and walk away from the murder and madness his other half is creating. Capo is a possessed killing machine, who thrives on shedding the blood of others. Death is his counselor and killing is his therapy, he spares no opportunity to take a life. Taral is a slave for Capo. Whatever he desires is her command. Struggling with her own demons, Taral is a crazed nympho seeking the attention from anyone who will have her. On the other side there is Charlene, Jay's wife. After seeing her husband being beat and dragged she went into a state of depression, not knowing that her curiosity sparked her husband's brutal attack. Follow these characters from the dirtiest and deadliest streets in Atlanta to the city's most patronized strip clubs. The lies, deceit and mayhem moves from coast to coast as the mystery behind Two Face and the sins of these four individuals unfold.

Keshawn Flower, also known as KeKe, is an 8 year old girl who was taken in by her grandparents. Though Compton, Ca. was where she resided the household and neighborhood in which she lived was far from ghetto. As a matter of fact it was close to perfection.

KeKe gets hit with devastating news and finds herself being forced to embrace the street life and take care of herself. Gang banging, dope selling, and numerous robberies are the highlights of her new life. It was go hard or go home and unfortunately there was no home.

The demon inside KeKe had turned into the Incredible Hulk. She flips the city upside down killing everything in sight. Rage is her new best friend and the streets are learning first hand what KeKe brings to the game.

Nikole, a high class call girl having been sent to Las Vegas as an incentive, meets a wealthy distinguished author, falls in love, marries him, and lives the life she always dreamed of until, "Block," her pimp from the past, comes for his "most lucrative investment." Determined to stay on top, Block threatens Nikole's new lifestyle with blackmail. Panicked Nikole must decide to either go along with a payoff or murder.

Skylar had everything a woman could hope for. She had the money, clothing, jewels and the perfect man to finance it all. She was living in the lap of luxury, until it all came crashing down after her boyfriend was murdered, during a drug deal gone wrong. Skylar suddenly finds herself broke, hungry, and alone. Unable to fend for herself, she leaves the world she once knew behind to start over in Atlanta and reclaim the man that once got away, Brian. Although, the two of them only shared a brief sexual encounter, Skylar never truly forgot the way Brian put it down, bringing her to the highest point of ecstasy. Not only will Brian be able to quench her sexual thirst, he's the perfect man to pull her out of her financial rut. Since their last encounter, Brian has been making his mark in the music industry, as one of the most sought after producers in the country. Skylar knows her life with Brian will be perfect, there's just one obstacle standing in her way, her cousin and Brian's fiancée', Lynn. While Lynn is planning the perfect wedding, Skylar is devising the perfect plan to steal her man. If Skylar has her way, "keeping it in the family", will be more than just a phrase.

Name: ______________________

Address: ______________________

City/State: ______________________

Zip: ______________________

ALL BOOKS ARE $10 EACH

QTY	TITLE	PRICE
	Essence of a Bad Girl	
	Executive Mistress	
	City Lights	
	A-Town Veteran	
	Beastmode	
	What We Won't Do for Love	
	Married to His Lies	
	Family Ties	
	Blocked In	
	Drama	
	Two Face	
	Dope, Death and Deception	
	Dealt the Wrong Hand	
	Shipping & Handling ($4 per book)	

TOTAL $ __________

To order online visit

www.gstreetchronicles.com

Send cashiers check or money order to:

G Street Chronicles

P.O. Box 490082 College Park, GA 30349